Design, Dance & Romance

De-ann Black

Text copyright © 2025 by De-ann Black
Cover Design & Illustration © 2025 by De-ann Black

All rights reserved.
No part of this book may be used or reproduced in any manner whatsoever without the written consent of the author.

This is a work of fiction. Names, characters, places, and incidents are either products of the author's imagination or are used fictitiously. Any resemblance to actual persons, living or dead, businesses, companies, events, or locales is entirely coincidental.

Paperback edition published 2025

Design, Dance & Romance

ISBN: 9798290730264

Design, Dance & Romance is the second book in the Dance, Music & Scottish Romance series set in Scotland.

Dance, Music & Scottish Romance series:
1. Romance Dancer
2. Design, Dance & Romance

Also by De-ann Black (Romance, Action/Thrillers & Children's books). See her Amazon Author page or website for further details about her books, screenplays, illustrations and artwork. www.De-annBlack.com

Romance:
Romance Dancer
Summer Ball Weddings & Waltzing
Quilt Shop by the Seaside
Embroidery Bee
Crafting Bee
Scottish Highlands New Year Ball
Ballroom Dancing Christmas Romance
Christmas Ballroom Dancing
Autumn Romance
Knitting & Starlight
Knitting Bee
The Sweetest Waltz
Sweet Music
Love & Lyrics
Christmas Weddings
Fairytale Christmas on the Island
The Cure for Love at Christmas
Vintage Dress Shop on the Island
Scottish Island Fairytale Castle
Scottish Loch Summer Romance
Scottish Island Knitting Bee
Sewing & Mending Cottage
Knitting Shop by the Sea
Colouring Book Cottage
Knitting Cottage
Oops! I'm the Paparazzi, Again
The Bitch-Proof Wedding
Embroidery Cottage
The Dressmaker's Cottage
The Sewing Shop

Heather Park
The Tea Shop by the Sea
The Bookshop by the Seaside
The Sewing Bee
The Quilting Bee
Snow Bells Wedding
Snow Bells Christmas
The Chocolatier's Cottage
Christmas Cake Chateau
The Beemaster's Cottage
The Sewing Bee By The Sea
The Flower Hunter's Cottage
Shed In The City
The Bakery By The Seaside
The Christmas Chocolatier
The Bitch-Proof Suit

Action/Thrillers:

Knight in Miami.
Agency Agenda.
Love Him Forever.
Someone Worse.
Electric Shadows.
The Strife of Riley.

Colouring books:
Summer Nature. Flower Nature. Summer Garden. Spring Garden. Autumn Garden. Sea Dream. Festive Christmas. Christmas Garden. Flower Bee. Wild Garden. Flower Hunter. Stargazer Space. Christmas Theme. Faerie Garden Spring. Scottish Garden Seasons. Bee Garden.

Embroidery books:
Floral Garden Embroidery Patterns
Floral Spring Embroidery Patterns
Christmas & Winter Embroidery Patterns
Sea Theme Embroidery Patterns
Floral Nature Embroidery Designs
Scottish Garden Embroidery Designs

Contents

Chapter One	1
Chapter Two	16
Chapter Three	31
Chapter Four	45
Chapter Five	59
Chapter Six	68
Chapter Seven	78
Chapter Eight	88
Chapter Nine	99
Chapter Ten	109
Chapter Eleven	122
Chapter Twelve	133
Chapter Thirteen	144
Chapter Fourteen	155
Chapter Fifteen	164
Chapter Sixteen	177
Chapter Seventeen	195
About De-ann Black	232

CHAPTER ONE

'The bakery was sold out of iced doughnuts, but I indulged in buying us yum yums.' Ferelith bounded into the theatre costume design shop carrying a bag of tasty treats and fresh milk for their morning tea break. She was so intent on sitting the bag down on the counter that she didn't notice the frantic hand waving from her sister, Wrae, alerting her they had a customer. And not just any customer. Ferelith was going to flip when she saw who was behind the curtain in the changing room, and about to emerge in all his gorgeous splendour.

'I was tempted by the tattie scones, but then I thought, no, go for the sticky yum yums,' Ferelith blethered on. 'I'll put the kettle on for tea.'

Ferelith was in her late twenties, wearing a summery floral print tea dress, and her long fiery red hair was pinned up in a messy ballet bun. She had a lovely pale complexion, like Wrae, and they both had green eyes, though Ferelith's were more peridot than emerald. In the past, she'd modelled part–time, and had slender curves, and long legs. The modelling work had boosted her income while she finished her fashion and design training.

Edinburgh was enjoying a warm, midsummer spell, and as a costume designer for the theatre, Ferelith loved making her own clothes, and mending vintage clothes to wear. She'd designed the summery tea dress to fit comfortably and wore it with ballet–style pumps for extra comfort, expecting to be on her feet all day again. Since coming to join Wrae in the family–owned costume design business, tucked in a cobbled niche in the heart of Edinburgh, style and comfort were her go–to outfits to wear in the shop.

If their busy schedule allowed, they aimed to make the most of the warmth of the summer that often lingered and blended with the amber glow of autumn.

Wrae was two years older than her sister, a classic beauty, similar in build, wearing a yellow shift dress, pumps, and a bumblebee wrist pincushion. She'd made it herself from fabric scraps, felt and an elastic wrist strap, and it was dotted with multi–coloured pin heads. And she'd made one for Ferelith, a robin rather than a bumble. Her auburn hair was swept up in a tidy bun, and she had a penchant for making her own clothes. The shift dress was one she'd made from her own pattern. She was supposed to be the sensible one, but grabbing two pieces of sparkling blue chiffon, off–cuts from the fairytale ballroom dress she was working on, she performed a sewing semaphore signal alert.

Ferelith noticed the impromptu performance, and sussed that there was something amiss, surmising that there was someone behind the curtain and she needed to button her lips about the buns.

Wrae was mid–signal, gesturing over towards the changing room that was on the opposite side of the room from the shop counter, when a hand whipped the curtain back to reveal himself. Not completely.

Mor wore tight–fitting black trousers. The fabric had a stretch in it and a scattering of sequins. The trousers emphasised the lean muscles of his long legs, and his shirt was more like a token gesture than an actual garment. See–through black fabric, cropped and unbuttoned. His six–pack was in full view.

Ferelith's world flipped as anticipated. He was one of the most handsome men she'd ever seen. Tall, fit, thirty, with thick blond hair, and azure blue eyes that were looking right at her. She'd seen videos of him perform ballroom, Latin, and stage dancing, and read about him in news features.

Originally from near Beinn Mhór in the Scottish Highlands, he was brought up in Edinburgh. His popularity was on the rise. And he was more than a little bit famous in the world of dance and entertainment.

'Mor is in for an emergency fitting,' Wrae announced. 'He has a photo–shoot this afternoon to promote his new dance show.'

Ferelith knew about the new show. They were making the costumes, and were on schedule with the designs. She hadn't met any of the cast as she'd only recently arrived back in Edinburgh to join Wrae in the business. Wrae had met all eight dancers cast in the show, including Mor, when they'd had their previous fittings for the costumes.

'This is my sister, Ferelith. She's joining me to work on the costume designs. She's just finished her latest course in fashion and design.'

He nodded, and his fabulous azure eyes held Ferelith's gaze for a second, sending her heart racing.

'Nice to meet you,' she said, trying to keep her voice steady, pleasant, as if she wasn't taken aback by the raw masculinity standing in front of her.

Pushing his elegant hands through his stylishly–cut hair, he brushed it back from his forehead. A few unruly strands refused to be tamed.

Then he raised his leg at full stretch in a strong balletic pose. 'When I do this, I need to be sure the trousers don't rip.'

Wrae had her pins at the ready. 'I can easily reinforce the seams. But there's plenty of stretch in the fabric. It's sturdier than it looks.'

He stretched again. 'Yes, nothing has pinged. But if you could strengthen the seams that would be great. The shirt fits fine.' His broad shoulders stretched underneath what fabric there was of it. 'I'll try on the next costume.' He disappeared behind the curtain.

Wrae swept Ferelith through to the back of the shop, to the kitchen, and closed the door so they wouldn't be overheard. They took the groceries with them.

'Before you say anything,' Wrae began, 'I didn't expect him to waltz in here this morning. But I couldn't refuse to help. He needs the outfits for the photo–shoot.'

'It's fine. I'm okay, I was just a wee bit thrown seeing him.'

'So was I when he walked in. But this is part of our world. We make extraordinary costumes for extraordinary and talented performers.'

'He. Is. Scrumptious,' Ferelith emphasised a little too loudly.

A demanding fist knocked on the kitchen door, startling them. Mor opened the door.

'Sorry to disturb your tea and yum yum break, but what do you think of my shirt?'

'We weren't having a tea break,' Ferelith was quick to tell him.

He frowned. 'I thought you said you were putting the kettle on for tea.'

'I did, I was, but I haven't done it yet.'

Ferelith wasn't sure if the look in his eyes was encouraging her to fill the kettle and start making the tea, or scolding her for dithering.

'So you're not making tea.' He sounded disappointed.

Ferelith filled the kettle and switched it on to boil. 'There. Would you like a cup?'

'I wouldn't say no. While it boils, what do you think of my shirt?' he repeated, unsure if he liked it. The black shirt had more fabric than the last one, but the style exposed his chest and the short sleeves showed his muscled arms.

'There's nothing wrong with the shirt,' said Ferelith. 'But you don't suit it. And it's the same colour as the first shirt. I'm assuming you want two different looks for the photos.'

'I do,' he said.

'Well, you need something different. Another colour, not black or dark tones,' Ferelith advised him. 'There are shirts hanging on one of the rails that might fit you.'

The three of them went back through to the rails and Ferelith picked out a sheer, red shirt. The fabric was shot through with scarlet sparkle.

His interest perked up. 'Can I try it on?'

Ferelith handed it to him, and he disappeared behind the curtain again.

Wrae glared at her sister.

What? Ferelith mouthed to her.

Wrae sighed and relented. It wasn't on their itinerary for the show's costumes, but maybe it would fit him. Their current schedule was busy, and with new shows being lined up for the coming weeks, their shop was thriving.

Since taking on the task of creating the costumes for Mor's dance show, it had brought quite a bit of extra business their way.

They'd taken over the business from their grandparents who'd retired and moved back up to the Scottish Highlands.

They specialised in costume design for theatres. There was another costume designer in the area whose costumes were vintage or pre–loved. Ferelith and Wrae's costumes were new.

The shop wasn't open to random customers, though few even knew the shop was there as it was tucked into a cobbled, hidden niche. The front window had a canopy shielding it from the sunlight. Flower pots filled with colourful blooms were making the most of the sunshine too. The heat had encouraged the pink, blue and yellow flowers to perk up, adding to the prettiness of the shop's exterior.

It had originally been a residential property before being converted for commercial purposes. Larger than it looked from the outside, it had an extensive room for the costume–making, and included a storeroom for costumes and fabric. A spare room, where the overspill of their work was tucked away, was nestled at the back that they used for all sorts of sundries. They'd retained the original kitchen, and often ate their meals there when they were on deadlines to finish costumes for customers.

Their grandparents had also given them the two–bedroom cottage they'd lived in for decades. Overspill of fabric and fashions from the shop made the cottage a creative hub as well as a cosy home.

But the shop was the core of their world. They both had their sewing machines set up on tables, plus there was a cutting table along one side of the room. And they each had a desk where they could draw their fashion illustrations and pattern designs for the clothes they made. The large, main room was painted light cream, creating a neutral backdrop for the colourful clothes they designed. Lit with spotlights, the room was the perfect hub for them to work on the theatre costumes.

Shelves were neatly stacked with bolts of fabric ranging from lycra and lace, to chiffon, silk, satin, velvet and all sorts of sequin and glittering fabric. Many of the fabrics had a stretch in them for the dance costumes.

Tucked in the corner was a mini haberdashery kitted out with sewing needles, scissors, thread, including embroidery thread, and ribbon and other trims.

Wrae had a vintage wooden sewing box, like a small chest of drawers, where she kept her own favourite sewing accoutrements, thread, particularly the silver grey and mid–grey thread that she used for the majority of her sewing as the colour blended into most fabrics.

Ferelith had brought her sewing basket with her. She'd had it for years, a gift from her grandmother, and it was filled with her preferred sewing needles, measuring tapes, scissors, thimble and thread. She liked the grey tones too, but also used a pale blue and a pale pink thread that she thought disappeared into many fabric colours, while enhancing them as well.

Wrae had always sketched her illustrations with a soft 2B pencil. Ferelith used a mechanical pencil as she never needed to sharpen it and this enabled her to create the fine details on her fashion drawings. They both used black ink, fine liner pens to draw the finished artwork. A few of their grandparents fashion illustrations were framed and hanging up on the walls. Wrae and Ferelith planned to add their own framed fashion drawings to the decor.

Ferelith rummaged through the rails of clothes for other suitable shirts, while Wrae checked the file that listed the agreed colours, theme and styling for the show's costumes. Red wasn't listed. Black, gold, silver and pastel tones were the base range.

He stepped out wearing the shirt. 'I like it. We're taking pictures for the promotional posters. This could look great.'

Ferelith gazed at the gorgeous man standing in front of her. A sizzling hot close–up of masculine temptation.

He suited the red shirt. The short sleeves displayed the lean muscles in his arms to full effect. And the fabric hugged the strong contours of his dancer's build. He wore it with another pair of black trousers that showed his long legs and slim hips to full effect. He looked like he belonged on the cover of a fashion or film magazine.

His handsome face with those blue eyes gazed right at her.

Her heart fluttered with excitement and trepidation. She'd meddled in the costume schedule, thrown another colour and design into the mix. Every change of garment affected the overall coordination of the show's theme.

Wrae bit her lip. 'The shirt and trousers are really flattering,' she admitted.

Mor performed a couple of stretches and dance moves while looking at himself in the full–length mirror. Not in a vain way, but assessing if the outfit would work for the photo–shoot. He nodded. 'This will be ideal for the photos.'

Then he viewed the shop, taking it in. The last time he'd been there it was busy with the other dancers having a fitting, and he hadn't appreciated it properly. 'It's a lovely shop. Do you run it by yourselves?'

'We do,' Wrae confirmed, summarising how they came to own it. 'Our grandmother was from the Scottish Highlands, and learned dressmaking from an early age. She moved to Edinburgh when she was a young woman, to pursue a career in making dresses, especially evening gowns, and ball gowns, party wear. She met and married a bespoke tailor. Our grandparents set up in business in the shop as costume designers for the theatre.'

'And your parents?' he prompted.

Ferelith replied. 'Our parents work for a fashion house in Edinburgh, so clothes, costumes are part of our upbringing. But they didn't want to take on this shop, preferring to work in mainstream fashion.'

'So we took it on,' said Wrae. 'I'd been working with my grandparents here for several years, learning the costume design business, as did Ferelith, though she's been away training in fashion and design and has only just come back to join me in the shop. We outsource machinists and others for jobs like sewing on sequins, time–consuming tasks that require thousands of sequins and beads to be sewn on the costumes.'

He nodded, taking this in, while putting on the classic black jacket that was part of his outfit.

Ferelith picked up the thread of their conversation. 'Mainly, we take on the design work and sew the costumes ourselves. We still use patterns that our grandparents designed.' She motioned to the numerous folders where the original pattern templates filled a shelf.

He walked over to look at them.

'The jacket you're wearing is made from one of my grandfather's original patterns,' said Ferelith. 'It's a favourite. Classic designs never go out of fashion. He designed it when he was a young man, around your age, and now here you are wearing it.'

'I like that,' said Mor.

'These are my patterns.' Wrae gestured to them. 'And Ferelith has brought her folders of designs.'

He admired the framed artwork on the walls. 'Are any of these fashion illustrations yours?' he said to them.

Ferelith shook her head. 'No, but we plan to add some of our inked illustrations to our grandparents' collection.'

Wrae opened a folder filled with her sketches for his show's costume designs. 'These are the original drawings of your costumes.'

Mor was eager to take a look, but was careful not to touch them so as not to smudge the black ink on the fine, artist quality white paper.

'Is that one of my outfits?' He peered at the sketch of his fashion figure wearing the sequined black trousers and a shirt.

'It is,' Wrae confirmed. Then she lifted Ferelith's folder up and opened it to show him her artwork for his show. 'We're different types of artists, and yet we both learned from our grandparents, so there is a style that we share.'

'I like both,' he said, unable to select a favourite, though there was an added artistry to Ferelith's illustration. He surmised that Wrae's drawings were closer to the pattern that would be made from the sketches, while Ferelith's merited being works of art in their own right. 'Would I be able to buy a couple of these illustrations?'

Ferelith and Wrae glanced at each other, unsure, as they'd never had anyone want to buy the sketches before, even though they were stylish pieces of fashion illustrations.

'I have spare sketches,' said Ferelith. She referenced them in her folder. 'These are variations on you wearing the sparkly black trousers, and an open–neck shirt.' The shirt fabric flowed artistically, while his long legs were emphasised by the elegant lines of the trouser design.

'I'd like to buy a couple of these.' He pointed to the two he was interested in.

Ferelith took them out of the folder and handed them to him. 'You can have them.'

Wrae gave him one of hers too. 'All the best with your forthcoming show.'

He was taken aback by their gesture.

'Thank you both so much,' he said. 'I'll have these framed and put up in my house.' He pictured having them in the living room, along with a framed copy of the poster that was due to be made from the pictures at the photo–shoot. A reminder of the show, something to look back on. Tickets for the new show were already selling well, and everyone from the dancers themselves to the show's director thought they had a success on their hands.

As taught to them by their grandparents, they'd signed their names on every finished piece of costume art. Wrae's signature was written with a flourish.

He studied Ferelith's name, barely legible, more like a design in itself, written below the fashion figure.

Ferelith took a large sheet of A3 white paper from a sketch pad, folded it in half, and put the sketches inside it to protect the ink from being smudged. Then she popped it in a large envelope.

Mor liked both their styles, and carefully took the gifted artwork with him into the changing room where he proceeded to change back into his original clothes, getting ready to leave the shop. He left the costume items on the hangers in the changing room.

'We'll tackle the alterations right away. They'll be ready in time for the photo–shoot,' Wrae assured him. She took the trousers over to her sewing machine and set it up ready to reinforce the trouser seams.

The kettle had long clicked off the boil, but Ferelith went through to the kitchen, while Wrae and Mor chatted, and made fresh tea. She swithered what to do about the yum yums, then opened the pack of four and put three of them on a plate.

Wrae popped into the kitchen and glanced at the tea. 'Mor takes milk, no sugar.' She looked at the yum yums. 'I doubt he'll take one, but it's polite to offer.'

Ferelith carried the tea tray through and sat it down on a table, well out of the way of any costumes or sewing work.

Mor stepped forward. 'Thank you.' He picked up a yum yum and took a bite.

Wrae and Ferelith glanced at each other, and then did likewise. For a few moments the room was chatter–free as they all munched the tasty treats.

He took a sip of his tea. 'The photos are being taken in the photographer's studio in Edinburgh at three this afternoon,' he told them. 'I'll drop by beforehand and pick the clothes up.'

'We'll have them ready to collect,' said Wrae. 'Ferelith models part–time and knows how busy a photo–shoot schedule can be.'

He looked at Ferelith, though not surprised that someone as lovely as her should be a model.

'I rarely model these days,' Ferelith explained. 'I'm concentrating on my costume design work.'

'What type of modelling is it you do?' he said, continuing the conversation when Ferelith would've preferred to talk about her sewing.

'Mainly photographic. To promote new clothing lines for magazine features and advertising. And a few runway assignments, modelling at fashion shows.'

'So you're experienced in fashion shoots,' he was quick to surmise. 'I don't suppose you'd be available to come along to the photo–shoot and offer to help me. I've never done a shoot like this where I'm the only one being photographed. And you could bring your sewing kit, in case something needs a minor repair during the shoot.'

Ferelith's first inclination was to refuse. She'd planned to help tackle the costumes. 'I was going to design another ballroom dress.'

'I can handle the shop myself this afternoon,' Wrae assured her, encouraging her to go. 'We'll have dinner at the eatery after you come back from the photo–shoot, and then we'll work on the costumes this evening.'

This was something that would help with their current busy schedule. The eatery was nearby and they could pop along instead of cooking dinner themselves.

'Okay,' Ferelith agreed.

He'd chosen Ferelith because of her modelling experience, glad she could be spared for a couple of hours from the shop. Her design skills were excellent.

It had nothing whatsoever to do with him feeling attracted to Ferelith and wanting to spend more time in her company, he lied to himself.

CHAPTER TWO

Ferelith lifted a bolt of pink glitter chiffon fabric down from a shelf and unrolled the required amount on the long cutting table, preparing it for the paper pattern pieces to be laid on.

Mor had left the shop, agreeing that he'd be back later to pick her up and drive them to the photographer's studio for the afternoon shoot.

Folding the fabric length–wise, ensuring it was the correct layout for the pattern, she pinned on the pieces for the skirt of the ballroom dress that would require a few layers of the light, sparkling fabric to create a fairytale effect when worn to dance on stage in the theatre. The bodice had already been cut from stretch velvet in a deep rose pink. The sleeves were fashioned from sheer stretch sparkle fabric in pale pink, and one of the sleeves was on a dolly, a flat cardboard arm shape, where most of the extra sequins had been sewn on or otherwise attached. The dolly allowed the fabric to be gently stretched so the sequins could be stitched on easily. The shop's mannequins were base body shapes, and sleeves were attached to the arm area of the dress once they were made. Many of the fabrics they used for the dancewear outfits had a stretch in them, and required careful prep work to create the beautiful costumes that suited the movement of the dancers when worn.

Movement was the key to all their designs, something learned from their grandparents. Everything began with how a dancer moved so that the costume enhanced the movements and didn't restrict them. Fabrics were chosen to flow lightly, often in sparkling chiffon or tulle, or sweep in swatches of silk and satin like the ballgown designs that were popular for performances. Fairytale–style ballgowns, like the one Ferelith was making, were a joy to design and sew. Wrae had put aside the blue ballgown she'd been working on to finish the work on Mor's items.

They'd both worked through lunch, still firing on the yum–yums from earlier, and snatched cups of tea to keep them going.

Wrae snipped the final threads from sewing the seams on Mor's trousers. 'There, all done.' She'd used her overlocker machine to help strengthen them too. Shaking them out, she hung them on a hanger along with the shirts, other pairs of trousers, and his jacket. Minor adjustments had been made, and more sparkle added to everything. Mor wanted to dazzle on stage. His expert dancing ensured he would even without the added sprinkling of sequins.

They both heard something drop through the letterbox. Wrae went to check what it was and came back with an envelope. 'We've already had the post this morning. This must have been hand delivered.'

Opening it, she pulled out two luxurious–looking invitations with gold embossed lettering, inviting them both to a ball for those in the performing arts industry.

'A ball! That sounds like fun, and a chance to meet other possible clients,' said Ferelith.

'And fancy I was just working on a ballgown of all things.'

They giggled and agreed they would attend.

'Do you want me to make you a snack and a cup of tea before Mor arrives?' Wrae offered, as Ferelith carefully cut the pattern pieces, placing each piece aside, ready for them to be assembled into the first phase of the ballgown.

Butterflies of excitement filled her adequately, and she wasn't sure why she felt so excited. She was only going along to the photo–shoot, something she was accustomed to. But with Mor. Every time she thought about him, her heartbeat increased, and she kept forcing herself to calm down. Yes, he was gorgeous. No, she'd never want to become involved with a man like him whose unsettled life wasn't one she wanted to be part of. She'd had enough broken hearts, broken promises and made silly choices when it came to dating. No way did she want to repeat those mistakes. Not that a heartbreaker like Mor would be interested in dating her she told herself.

'I'll book a table for us at the eatery for five tonight,' Wrae said, heading through to make the tea. She kept the kitchen door open and chatted while she filled the kettle and set the cups up. 'There's a yum yum going spare,' she reminded Ferelith. 'Do you want it to keep you going until dinner?'

'No, I'm fine.'

'You don't sound fine. You sound keyed–up. Not that I blame you. Mor is a handsome one.'

'We agreed we wouldn't get embroiled in any foolish romances with our clients,' Ferelith reminded her.

'Chance would be a fine thing,' Wrae scoffed, cutting the yum yum in two to split it between them for their tea break. She poured two mugs of tea and carried them through on a tray along with a plate with the half yum yums.

Ferelith laughed, picked up a half and bit into it.

Wrae ate the other half.

They drank their tea and chatted about their current predicament.

'I'm not going to make a habit of being on hand at publicity shoots or rehearsals for Mor's show,' Ferelith said firmly. 'Our grandparents never did things like that. It was always quite professional, everything handled with aplomb and attentiveness in the shop. Occasionally, they'd attend the theatre rehearsals, but that was only when significant changes were needed to the costumes for a show.'

'I agree. But this sounds like a one–off obligement.'

They were finishing their tea, when Efie buzzed herself into the shop, using the keypad code outside the frontage. In her latter years, she was a lifelong expert in dressmaking and costume design, preferring to work from home and pop into the shop to drop off and collect garments for sewing.

'It's just me,' Efie announced cheerily, laden with two large bags brimming with dresses she'd been finishing, sewing on beads and sparkles by hand. The dresses looked like they were making a bid to escape from the bags, and Wrae hurried over and grabbed one off her.

They put the bags down on a table.

'All done,' said Efie. 'I'll be seeing sparkles in my sleep, but I know this is a rush job, so...'

'Thank you, Efie,' Wrae said, grateful to be able to outsource work like this. Efie had worked for their grandparents and they'd continued the association, as they had with several long–time dressmakers and machinists like Efie.

'They say that most actors and stage performers don't retire,' said Efie. 'I'd like to include dressmakers like me. I wouldn't know what to do with myself anyway. My fingers are always itching to start stitching after a few days off.' She looked around at the organised busy vibe of the shop. 'What are the two of you up to today?'

They told her.

'Mor! Oh, he's a handsome man. And such a talented dancer. I'm going to get tickets for his show. I love dance shows, especially when we've had a hand in making the costumes.'

They chatted about the show while working on bits and pieces of the costumes.

A mannequin wore a calico toile, a mock–up of one of the dresses that Ferelith had designed. A toile enabled them to make an inexpensive calico version of the pattern, and any alterations could be made to the design before the pattern was cut from the intended fabrics such as silk, chiffon and satin.

Ferelith had put aside the ballgown pieces to work on them later, and pinned and adjusted the calico toile. The dress was for one of the show's tango numbers, and was cut on the bias to accentuate the shape of the asymmetrical design that included a thigh–high split and varying lengths of the hemline.

Another dress based on the same type of pattern hung on a mannequin, already finished apart from the sparkling stretch fringing that needed trimmed to size. The stretch fringing moved well when worn, especially for fast–paced dances with lots of spins and kicks. Wrae checked the lengths required, and began to measure and trim the fringing as they spoke about Mor's dance prowess.

'I've never seen Mor perform live on stage,' said Ferelith. 'But I've watched plenty of video clips of his dancing. He's strong and balletic. There's something about his dancing that's quite mesmerising.'

'I saw him dance last year during his tour,' said Efie. 'It was a one–night performance in Edinburgh as part of his whirlwind tour of various theatres. He was magnificent. The other dancers were excellent, but Mor has a light about him that makes him stand out on stage.'

'Star quality,' Wrae summarised.

'Exactly,' Efie agreed, while sewing a strip of sequins on to one of the costumes. An expert in sequin and bead work, she started to make short work of the sequins needing added to a dress. Like many of the dresses for the show, it had a leotard base with a skirt attached, and was then sewn with sequins and other trims.

'Mor told me his dance tour was so successful that one of the theatres approached him to design a show for them,' said Wrae. 'Instead of touring and doing one or two–night performances in various cities and towns, the show will be on for a full run at the theatre throughout the autumn.'

'It'll probably be less tiring than having to travel for weeks on the tour,' said Efie.

'That's what Mor said to me,' Wrae added. 'And it enables them to have more lavish sets as it's only in one theatre. We're designing the costumes with the atmosphere of the sets in mind. It'll be quite spectacular.'

The shop's buzzer interrupted their conversation. Wrae checked the monitor and blinked. 'It's Mor.'

Ferelith checked the time. 'He's early!' In a mild panic, she started to grab her things, stuffing her sewing kit into a quilted tote bag she'd made. 'I'm not ready.'

Wrae gave Ferelith a head start to run through to the back of the shop, and then buzzed him in.

'You look lovely, Ferelith,' Efie called after her as she disappeared into a spare room that they used for all sorts of sundries.

Hurrying to get ready, Ferelith ran a brush through her hair and touched up her lipstick. Her heart thundered with a mix of mild panic and excitement. Calm down, she mentally scolded herself. This wasn't a date, it was business, even though the excitement level felt like a first date.

'I know I'm a bit early,' Mor admitted as he walked in. His tall, broad–shouldered stature seemed to fill the room. 'But I thought Ferelith and I could head to the photographer's studio ahead of time and maybe discuss any tips she can offer me.'

'She'll be through in a minute,' Wrae assured him.

Ferelith took a deep breath and walked through giving Mor a pleasant smile and hoping she looked outwardly calm.

The way he smiled at her sent a charge of extra excitement through her, testing her resolve to hide her reaction. He wore expensive black trousers and a silk–back waistcoat over his open–neck pale blue shirt. If this was his attempt to look businesslike, he'd overshot the mark. She thought he looked even more handsome than when she'd seen him earlier.

Wrae introduced Efie to him.

'This is Efie, she helps us with the sequin and bead work for the costumes.'

Efie fluffed up her silvery blonde curls and adjusted her cardigan. 'I'm thrilled to meet you, Mor. I saw your show last year. It was fantastic. My husband and I were there. We had a great night out at the theatre.'

'I'm pleased you liked the show, Efie,' he replied politely, wondering if she wanted to have a photo taken with him. He was accustomed to people wanting this and was always happy to oblige.

Efie did want a photo with him, but didn't intend to ask him while he was there on business.

'I'm going to see your new show,' Efie added.

'I don't have any guest tickets organised yet,' he said. 'But I do have backstage passes.' He dug two passes out from his pocket and handed them to Efie.

'These are great!' Efie said to him. 'I hope I can get a photo backstage with you on the night.'

'Yes, the meet and greet guests will be there getting pictures taken with me. But would you like one now, in case it's busy on the night?' he offered.

Efie's face lit up with an eager smile. 'I certainly would.' She stood beside him and snapped a couple of pictures with her phone.

Mor had his arm around Efie's shoulder, leaned in and smiled for the photos.

'Thank you, Mor, these are wonderful,' Efie enthused.

Ferelith and Wrae were pleased that their friend was happy.

'Should we take a group photo while we're all here?' he suggested.

Wrae jumped at the chance. 'We'll put it up on our website.'

Gathering together, he used his phone to take the pictures. He sent them all copies. Efie also took a picture of him with his arms around Ferelith and Wrae's shoulders as he stood sandwiched between them showing their sewing machines in the background.

'I spoke to my show director about the red shirt,' Mor said to Ferelith and Wrae. 'He likes the bold colour and wonders if we can add splashes of red to some of the costumes to make them blend in with the addition of red to the theme.'

'Yes, we can do that,' Wrae told him.

'I'll discuss some ideas we have in mind with you on the way to the photographer's studio,' he said to Ferelith.

'Great.' Ferelith tried to sound chirpy but calm, and wasn't sure she'd hit the right note. She glanced at Wrae on the way out as Mor escorted her from the shop. It was a look that said — what a pickle I've got myself into.

Wrae and Efie waved them off.

'I could be wrong,' Efie confided, 'but I sensed a spark between them.'

Wrae nodded thoughtfully. 'So did I.'

Outside in the sunshine, Mor led her to his expensive white car. She was aware that she barely came up to his shoulders, and that his hair looked golden blond in the bright sunlight. His intense azure eyes were the bluest she'd ever seen in real life, though there was a dreamlike quality to her current situation.

She'd expected a busy day sewing ballgowns and costumes, after having a morning tea break with Wrae, not having this gorgeous dancer politely open the passenger door of his car and getting into his world of glitz and publicity.

Mor drove them off through the busy city.

As they drove past the nearby eatery, the traffic paused, giving Ferelith a chance to peer out the window at the eatery's menu board that was outside the premises.

Mor followed her eyeline. 'Feeling peckish?'

'No, just wondering what's on the menu. I'm meeting Wrae for dinner there this evening around five.'

'I haven't been in it since the premises was refurbished when the new owner took over. I was away on tour at the time last year. I've heard he kept the original piano in the restaurant area and customers are welcome to sit and play it while others dine.'

'Yes, that's what Wrae tells me. I haven't been in it yet either.' She glanced again at the menu before he joined in the flow of traffic again. 'The menu looks tasty.' She was looking forward to a relaxing dinner with Wrae after what would surely be a tense but intriguing time with Mor at the photo–shoot.

Mor continued to drive them through Edinburgh. The historic architecture of the city was highlighted against the cobalt sky, particularly the majestic Edinburgh castle in the distance.

'How long have you been here?' he said.

'Only since Wrae first took on the job of creating the costumes for your show.'

He remembered the initial meeting at the costume shop with Wrae. His show director, the theatre producer, and the eight dancers that had just been announced as part of the new show were there as well, discussing the feasibility of designing the show's costumes. The shop had been gaining high praise in the dance and theatre circles, and the meeting went so well that Wrae secured the contract. He remembered too that Wrae informed them that her sister, an expert in fashion and design, and costume work, would be shortly joining her and that they'd both tackle the work. Her comment added reassurance to the deal, and everyone was happy to push ahead with the plans.

'The timing was ideal,' Ferelith told him. 'I'd just finished my fashion and design course in Glasgow, and had moved back home to Edinburgh. Our grandparents had retired and left us the shop and their cottage on the outskirts of the city. They've moved back up north to the Scottish Highlands. My grandmother says it feels right, as if life has gone full circle, back to her original home in the Highlands. My grandfather loves it up there too. And he has relatives in Aberdeen so they visit the city there regularly.'

Feeling as if she'd revealed enough, she brought the conversation back to Mor and his show. 'The theme of the show sounds interesting. The brief from your show director described it as a romantic adventure.'

'It is. A romantic adventure played out through dance.' He heard himself sound like the line from their proposed poster advertising the show and redirected the focus of the conversation.

'I brought a few changes of clothes with me.' Mor thumbed to the bags in the back seat.

She noticed he was clean shaven, looked showered and fresh, and there was a sensual hint of bergamot from his subtle aftershave. In profile, his sculptured features were as handsome as face on. He was probably photogenic she assessed.

'What type of picture do you want for the poster?'

'My show director wants something dynamic. That's why the addition of red into the costume's colour theme sparked his interest. And mine. We're having to put the show together quite quickly. He wants a different show than the one we had on tour.'

'That makes sense. Anyone who has seen the previous show and enjoyed it, will likely want to come along to see something new.'

'The dance rehearsals are going well. I'm still honing the choreography. We practise at the dance studio that's near your shop.'

The studio was fairly new and since its opening earlier in the year, it had become popular with those wanting to use the two main rooms — the dance room and the stage room.

The dance room had a sprung floor, a barre along one wall for stretching, and a mirrored wall. It was popular for dance show rehearsals and choreography work. The stage room included a sprung floor too, and a stage for rehearsal use. It included a well–tuned piano for performance practise. The stage had excellent lighting effects that made it ideal for rehearsing stage show performances.

The photographer's studio wasn't too far away, and soon Mor pulled up outside the premises and they headed inside. Although Ferelith offered to help carry one of Mor's costume bags, he insisted on lugging everything himself, though considering his strength, it didn't seem a hard task.

The same type of excitement that Ferelith always felt when walking into a professional studio set up with lights, backdrops and equipment, ignited in her as she ventured into the brightly lit studio with Mor.

'We're slightly early,' Mor admitted to the photographer, a man in his mid–thirties, busy setting up his cameras for the shoot.

'Early is fine,' the photographer said with a welcoming smile. 'The changing room is through there.' He gestured to a room off the studio.

Mor nodded and disappeared into the room taking the costume bags with him.

'Are you part of Mor's stage management? Or publicity?' the photographer said pleasantly to Ferelith. 'Or girlfriend?' Used to watching people through the telltale eye of a lens, he'd acquired a knack for seeing connections that would otherwise be missed. Joining the dots between Mor and Ferelith, he'd seen a glimpse of romance between them.

'No, I'm Ferelith, Mor's costume designer.'

The photographer's interest sparked even more. 'Excellent. My stylist is off today, so I'd welcome your assistance with Mor's look for the pics.'

Ferelith smiled tightly as she felt the nervous butterflies swoop in again. 'Happy to help.'

'Just go through to the changing room and help Mor get dressed for the first round of shots with the red shirt and black trousers.' He checked the updated notes the show director had messaged him.

Another tight smile hid her urge to make a run for it before she became embroiled in being Mor's dresser.

He stepped out from behind a curtain wearing black trousers and a black shirt.

'Wrong outfit,' Ferelith informed him. 'The photographer wants to start with the red shirt ensemble.'

'Right.' Mor was used to quick changes during dance shows, and lacked any sense of propriety when it came to stripping off his shirt in front of her, revealing a wall of sexy muscles.

She felt a blush rise in her cheeks, due to compete with the bright scarlet of the shirt he was now rummaging through the costumes to find.

Clasping the shirt in one hand, he turned to her. 'Should I whip off these black trousers and jump into the pair that goes with this shirt?'

In an alternative universe, where her reputation wouldn't be affected by scandalous behaviour, her reply could've been a whole lot different.

'Yes,' she said, walking over to another part of the changing room while he stripped down to his boxers.

She tried not to look at his honed physique reflected in the multiple mirrors in the changing room that made her feel she was in the midst of a kaleidoscope. But perhaps not hard enough. Shame on her, she thought, wondering what else was in store for her being Mor's makeshift stylist.

CHAPTER THREE

'Do that spin again,' the photographer encouraged Mor, while taking numerous pictures in front of the studio backdrop. An assistant changed the colour of the backdrop, and more pictures were taken of Mor, wearing the red shirt and black trousers, dancing and posing for the shots.

Mor glanced at Ferelith, gauging her reaction.

She smiled and nodded. The red shirt had started slightly open at the neck, but was now fully unbuttoned. The momentum of Mor's spins caused the lightweight, silky fabric to billow around him, and she imagined that some of these shots would be quite artistic. Perhaps one would become the main photo for the poster.

While the backdrop was changed again, Mor ran over to Ferelith. 'What do you think? Any tips?'

'I've obviously not seen the picture previews, but from watching the movements, I think you've probably got some winning shots in the bag,' she said.

The photographer adjusted two of the large spotlights and other equipment, altering them to reflect and diffuse the lighting.

'I'll take a few more of you wearing the red shirt,' the photographer called over to Mor. 'Then change into your next costume, and we'll run through the routine again. Take a look at these.' He beckoned to Mor and Ferelith to take a peek at the preview images on his camera.

Mor smiled, surprised how well the images had captured the essence of the dancing. 'These are excellent.'

Ferelith agreed.

'Let's go again,' the photographer said, keeping the pace lively.

Mor repeated the sequence of dance movements that included spins, kicks and balletic poses.

Then Mor hurried through to get changed into the black shirt and trousers, and another set of pictures were taken.

Viewing them together, the three of them agreed that the first costume was more dynamic. Mor then put on a waistcoat without a shirt. Another round of photos followed.

'We need pictures for various publicity purposes,' Mor explained to the photographer. 'I'd like copies of the pictures that include all the changes in costume.'

'Can do,' the photographer said, sounding pleased that the shoot had gone well.

Mor had danced for practically the whole session, but Ferelith felt that her heart had experienced a workout too from seeing Mor perform. She hid her reaction to him so well that he didn't know if she was attracted to him or not. They got on well, he thought, and he was comfortable in her company. He certainly found her attractive, but any thoughts of romance weren't on his schedule. He was determined to focus all his energies on getting the show ready in time for the opening night. The summer sun showed no hint of autumn, but he knew that his hectic schedule would soon speed up and that summer would merge with autumn's glow so quickly that there would be no time for romance.

Walking outside into the warm glow of the late afternoon, Mor carried all his bags and put them in the car. Ferelith sat in the passenger seat.

Mor wore his white shirt and waistcoat, but there was no mistaking his underlying dancer's fit build as he sat beside her and started up the car. Pulling out into the flow of traffic, he drove them back into the heart of the city while they chatted.

'I'll drive you back to your shop,' he said.

Ferelith checked the time. Quarter to five. 'Could you drop me at the eatery? It'll be five by the time we get there. I promised I'd meet Wrae for dinner.'

'Yes,' he said, happy to oblige, almost wishing he could join them. Now that the photo–shoot was over, any tension he'd felt about it had gone, and his appetite had kicked–in.

'Are you rehearsing this evening?' Ferelith said, making polite conversation.

'I am. At the dance studio,' he elaborated. 'We're practising the new choreography for Act Two of the dance show.'

'It sounds like quite an entertaining show with various types of dance routines.' She'd heard him talking about this to the photographer, describing the storyline that mixed plenty of romance with adventure.

'There's everything from ballroom to Latin numbers, ceilidh dancing and modern stage choreography,' he confirmed. 'We're working on the tango, and the ceilidh routine.'

'Are you wearing a kilt? Wrae said you'd yet to decide.'

'I think I will. The ceilidh number is dynamic and fast–paced, and I think the kilt would look great.'

'She said you had a kilt, but it's a traditional design and if you wore it for the show, you'd want us to sparkle it up.'

'I'm sure you'd make a fine job of adding some glitz.'

Ferelith nodded. 'We certainly could.'

The amber glow of the fading sun made the Edinburgh sky look like burnished gold, and highlighted the castle and other buildings beautifully.

Mor pulled up outside the eatery. 'I appreciate everything you've done to help me today.' He cast her an unintentional sexy smile.

'I'm glad to have helped.' She got out of the car, feeling her heart react to him.

'Enjoy your dinner,' he called to her and then drove off.

Ferelith took a steadying breath, feeling like she'd been in the whirlwind of Mor's day, and was now looking forward to relaxing and having dinner with Wrae.

Walking into the calm atmosphere of the eatery, she received a warm welcome from the new owner, a man in his early thirties. Fairly tall and fit, his hair was auburn and his eyes hazel. He wore his chef whites, without the hat. Only a couple of tables were occupied, but the eatery was due to become busy with those arriving for dinner. Since its reopening after the refurbishment, that included extending the small function room through the back of the premises to provide a larger dance floor, it had become even more popular. A poster on the doorway leading through from the dining and bar area to the function room advertised a forthcoming ceilidh dance party night.

He showed Ferelith to her pre–booked table. Wrae hadn't arrived yet, but Ferelith knew she'd be there on time. 'I'm slightly early.'

'Can I offer you a drink? Wine? Soft drink? Tea?'

'Tea, please.'

'Busy day,' he surmised from her tone.

'Hectic and unexpectedly exciting.'

'A lively mix,' he said with a warm smile. 'I'll bring a pot of tea over. Make yourself comfortable.' He gestured to the beautiful dark wood piano that was part of the fittings and available for customers to play. 'Or tinkle the keys while I make it. If you play.' He was fishing for information. 'Do you play?'

Tell the truth? Or smile and brush over her ability? If she still had it.

'Ferelith is a wonderful pianist,' Wrae's voice broke into the conversation as she arrived and sat down at the table. Wrae had dined there a few times, and was familiar with the new proprietor.

Lochlen looked interested.

'My sister has recently joined me in the costume design shop,' Wrae told him.

'Maybe you'd regale us with a tune.' His handsome face smiled at Ferelith. 'I'm Lochlen, I recently took over the eatery. I've kept the piano, but restyled some of the decor. I don't play very well myself.'

'I'm well out of practise,' Ferelith admitted, not wanting to get his hopes up.

He gestured again to the piano. 'Then this is a fine time to practise before you have dinner.' Lochlen left them to decide and went over to the bar to talk to his staff as they got ready for the influx of diners.

'Do play something,' Wrae encouraged her. 'I'd love to hear you play again. It's been so long.'

'What do you want me to play?' said Ferelith, sitting down at the piano that was near their table.

'One of those lovely sonatas. They're so romantic. And calming. I need to unwind from the busy afternoon. Then you can tell me all about the photo–shoot with Mor.'

Lochlen overheard the name and chimed–in the conversation from the bar area where he made them a pot of tea for two. 'Mor, the dancer?'

'Yes, we're designing the costumes for Mor's new show,' said Wrae. 'It's on at one of the theatres in Edinburgh throughout the autumn.'

'I must buy a ticket,' he said.

'Do you dance?' Ferelith said to him as he carried the tea over on a tray.

'Not to Mor's level. I can handle a social waltz, and ceilidh dancing, but that's all. I enjoy going to the theatre, and there are so many options for entertainment here in the city.'

He left Wrae to peruse the menu while Ferelith sat at the piano.

Ferelith let her hands run over the keys, starting to play the gentle introduction to the sonata.

Other customers came in for dinner, and several tables started to fill up as an influx of them arrived for their meal. Hearing Ferelith play the piano, she had an interested and appreciative small audience.

Lochlen and his staff served the diners while taking in the melody that added to the relaxing mood of the eatery.

Ferelith finished playing part of a sonata, and sat back down at the table with Wrae.

'You play so beautifully,' said Wrae, sounding a bit emotional hearing her sister play the piano again. 'It reminds me of years ago.'

Hearing the wistfulness in Wrae's voice, she assured her that she was happy with her career choice. 'I'm happy working on the costume designs. Truly I am.'

'That was exquisite,' Mor said, taking them aback. They hadn't noticed him arriving with the other diners, and he'd heard Ferelith play the sonata. 'I danced to that song once during a stage performance. It's a beautiful piece of music, and you played it so well.'

Ferelith felt a blush start to rise across her cheeks. 'Thank you. I'm well out of practise.'

'I'd never have guessed,' said Mor. 'Have you played professionally?'

'No.' Ferelith didn't elaborate.

Wrae picked up on his interest and was pleased to tell him about her sister's past. 'Ferelith attended piano lessons when she was a wee girl, and had at one time considered a career in musical theatre. She attended stage school.'

Mor blinked. 'Musical theatre?' He sounded interested.

Ferelith shrugged off the part of her life she'd left behind in what seemed like a lifetime ago before she'd concentrated only on her fashion design training. 'It was a wild dream. I thought I'd like to work in musical theatre. I loved going to see various shows in the theatre when I was a wee girl, and I considered being part of that world.'

'What made you give it up?' Mor said to her.

'As I'm sure you know, you need a combination of talents in acting, singing and dancing, or at least two of those,' Ferelith explained. 'I wasn't any good at acting. I can play piano, but my singing isn't great, or my dancing. By the time I realised this, I'd already been sewing and dressmaking for years, as had Wrae. So I decided to follow my love of fashion and design.' She shrugged. 'And here I am.'

Ferelith didn't sound downcast. But Mor felt a pang of sadness for her. He knew how much he'd miss dancing and performing on stage.

'We used to make ballgowns and evening dresses for our dolls when we were wee girls, and put on dolls' fashion shows at home for our friends,' Wrae told Mor.

'I love designing and making costumes,' Ferelith said to him, her eyes shining with the joy her work brought her. 'And I get to make dazzling costumes for people like you.' She smiled at Mor, melting his heart a little.

'Mor! I'm about to order dinner,' a woman called over to him, interrupting their conversation. In her late twenties, she was similar in height and build to Ferelith, with light brown hair swept up in a soigné chignon, and ice blue eyes. Her clothes were casual chic and flattered her slender but shapely figure.

Mor nodded that he'd be right over. Then he smiled at Ferelith and Wrae. 'Well, I'll leave you to enjoy your dinner.' He looked at Ferelith. 'I hope you'll play something else this evening.'

Ferelith smiled, without committing to this, and glanced at the lovely young woman whose company he headed back to.

'That's Torra,' Wrae confided. 'She's one of the dancers involved in Mor's show. And she's his leading lady. In the show,' she added quickly. 'I don't know if they're dating or have been a couple in the past.'

Somehow, seeing Mor with Torra, Ferelith felt an ache in her heart. This reaction took her aback far more than the surprise of Mor being there for dinner.

'The blue ballgown I was making this afternoon is for her to wear for waltzing with Mor towards the end of the show,' Wrae added.

Ferelith pictured Torra wearing the dress, dazzling on stage. 'I'm sure she'll look wonderful.'

'When she tried the dress on in the shop during one of the fittings, it suited her really well,' said Wrae. Then she picked up the menu and changed the conversation, eager to hear all about the photo–shoot.

They ordered the cottage pie that was topped with mashed potato and served with a mix of fresh vegetables.

Ferelith told Wrae what happened at the photographer's studio. 'I didn't know where to look when he was getting changed. There were mirrors everywhere.'

Wrae giggled. 'It sounds like you had a fun time with Mor.'

'I did. Though I have no intention of getting involved with him if that's what you're thinking.'

It was what Wrae was thinking. Though she didn't want Ferelith's heart to be broken if she had a fling with Mor. He didn't seem like the type to want to settle down, and his busy career certainly wouldn't provide much chance of that.

'Mor's a heartbreaker,' Ferelith said clearly. 'And I'm not looking for romance. Not yet. I want to work on the costume designs.'

Wrae nodded that she understood.

They continued to enjoy their dinner, but Ferelith noticed Lochlen glancing over at Wrae a few times.

'I notice Lochlen keeps looking over at you.'

'Does he?'

'You know he does.'

'Okay, so perhaps I've seen him glancing over,' Wrae relented. 'But I'm in the same mind as you when it comes to romance.' She sighed heavily. 'I feel that you've only just arrived to join me in the shop, and this is the start of us building our costume design business together. We're thriving at the moment, and with these new theatre and dance shows, I sense we're going to do really well. I do want to marry and settle down one day, but not yet, and certainly not in the middle of us being so busy.'

'I agree,' Ferelith said, making it clear that she was in total agreement. 'Romance would complicate our plans.'

Wrae looked at her with a serious expression. 'But, if either of us meets the right man, falls deeply in love, and there's a true chance of real romance, we choose love and happiness above all else.' She lifted up her cup of tea.

Ferelith lifted her cup up too. They tipped them in a sisterly toast, and a promise, as they had done since they were young girls.

Having had her day cast to the wind by helping Mor, even though romance wasn't in the mix, Ferelith had experienced how her schedule could be easily affected by being involved with him outwith the costume shop. Here she was having dinner at the eatery with Wrae, as a treat and to save time cooking dinner, in order to catch up with the work she'd missed doing that afternoon. Their schedule was tight but doable, except when something else was thrown into the mix to set them off kilter.

Mor flicked a glance across the room at Ferelith and Wrae, wondering what they were toasting, as he ate his breaded fish and salad.

'...and I'd like you to add more lifts into the second half of tonight's routine.' Torra's voice broke into Mor's faraway thoughts. She continued to eat her lemon risotto.

'Yes, I've a few changes to the choreography in mind, especially the lifts,' he agreed.

'Ah, so this is where the two of you have been hiding,' Creag said, approaching their table and feeling himself welcome to sit down and join them at their table. In his early thirties, tall, well–dressed, with a fit dancer's build, he motioned over to one of the staff, indicating he wanted to order dinner.

Creag was one of the show's lead male dancers, and was partnered with Torra too when the storyline of their dance show required it. He hadn't been in the eatery since its refurb.

His rich chestnut hair had a ruffling of curls that he'd long given up trying to tame. Keen blue eyes flicked from Mor to Torra, encouraging them to include him in their chat.

'I was just saying to Mor that we should practise more lifts in tonight's choreography,' Torra said to Creag.

'My thoughts entirely,' Creag agreed. 'Far better to be overly dramatic than underplay what we're all capable of. At least I am.'

'I am too,' Torra was quick to chip–in.

A member of staff handed Creag a menu. Glancing at it, he then eyed the risotto. 'That looks tasty. I'll have this.' He ordered the risotto and handed back the menu. The staff member went away to get his order.

Mor ate his fish while Creag paid most of his attention to Torra.

Torn between the feelings Creag had for her, and waiting for the right moment to ask her out on a date, his usual casual character was always more restless when he was in her company. And with the rehearsals for the show now due to throw them together practically every day, he was more edgy than ever.

Torra, thinking of Creag as no more than a dance partner, didn't notice.

But Mor had picked up on the vibe lately, since offering one of the principal roles to Creag.

While they chatted, Creag noticed Mor looking over at the other side of the restaurant, and followed his line of vision. 'I see Wrae is here having dinner,' he remarked.

'Yes, she's with her sister, Ferelith,' Mor told him. 'She's a costume designer too, working at the shop.'

'Ferelith seems very nice,' Creag remarked.

'She is,' Mor confirmed strongly. He told them about the photo–shoot, and that red was being added into the colour theme for the show's costumes.

'Can I have a red waistcoat?' Creag requested. 'I saw one hanging up on a rail in the costume shop during a fitting. It's probably gone by now, but if not, I'd like it for one of the ceilidh or Latin numbers.'

'I'd love a red dress for the tango routine,' Torra added.

'You'd look sensational,' said Creag.

'I'll tell Ferelith and Wrae,' Mor assured them.

A call came through for Mor from his show director.

'We're going with one of the red shirt pictures for the main poster,' he said to Mor.

'Great. And Creag and Torra want more red in their costumes.'

'Go ahead and organise that with Wrae and her sister,' said the director. 'Do it fast. I've some interviews lined up with the press and media to promote the show.'

'I'm having dinner with Torra and Creag in the eatery, not far from the dance studio where we're rehearsing at seven this evening. Ferelith and Wrae are dining here. I'll tell them.'

'Do that,' the director encouraged him. 'The ticket sales are doing great, but the theatre's producer wants to secure all the dates. We especially want a full–house on the opening week of the dance show.'

'I'll go over and talk to them right now,' said Mor.

CHAPTER FOUR

Finishing the call, without finishing his dinner, Mor walked over to Ferelith and Wrae's table. They'd eaten their first course and were contemplating having pudding.

'I can recommend Lochlen's raspberry cheesecake,' Wrae was telling Ferelith when Mor approached them.

'Sorry to intrude on your dinner,' he said. 'But I've just had a call from my show director. The picture for the poster has been chosen. A red shirt one. Torra wants a red dress now for the tango routine, and Creag says he'd like to wear the red waistcoat he saw hanging up on a rail in your shop if it's available.'

'The waistcoat is still there,' said Wrae. 'It was a prototype design for the black one you're going to wear for the show. I'll put it aside for him.'

'We have gorgeous red fabric in stock. Ruby red chiffon, scarlet silk and tulle,' Ferelith told him. 'There's a short, flirty pink dress that was made for Torra. I have the pattern, and could make a version in red.'

'Excellent,' Mor sounded relieved that they made no fuss about him changing the costume schedule.

'I'll make a start on cutting the pattern pieces for the dress tonight,' Ferelith told him.

'Working late at the costume design shop?' Lochlen said to Ferelith and Wrae, overhearing the conversation as he approached to take their pudding order.

Mor didn't miss the friendly accusation in Lochlen's tone that he was causing them to work overtime on the show's costumes.

'Yes, so we'll indulge in having pudding to keep us going,' Wrae said, not picking up on the underlying tone of Lochlen's comment.

Ferelith sensed a change in the atmosphere, not in a bad way, but in a well–meaning way.

'I've taken up a lot of their time today,' said Mor, looking the chef in the eyes, wondering if it was Ferelith or Wrae that had brought out the protective instinct in Lochlen.

From unintentionally hearing snippets of Ferelith and Wrae's conversation over dinner while he went back and forth attending to the diners, Lochlen had pieced together a patchwork of their day. It seemed that Mor had them buzzing around to his tune, even though they seemed quite accommodating.

Lochlen knew what it was like to work long hours and have your busy schedule added to because someone else put their career's priorities first. He didn't know Mor, but from first impressions, he seemed like a man used to being admired and accommodated. Acknowledging the dancer's talent and own achievements from hard work, he nonetheless hoped that Mor wouldn't encroach too much on their free time. He also acknowledged it was none of his business, but he had a tendency to interfere, especially when scenarios were playing out in his eatery.

'I'm looking forward to seeing your show,' Lochlen added to Mor, taking the edge of the tense atmosphere. 'It'll be extra interesting knowing that the costumes were made by Wrae and Ferelith.'

'Are you a performer yourself?' Mor said to Lochlen.

'No, I have enough drama running the eatery and creating new menus I hope people will enjoy,' Lochlen told Mor. 'And I have the new ceilidh dance nights to organise. Come along and dance a jig or a reel if you have a night off.' He didn't expect Mor to take him up on his offer.

'I'll do that,' Mor said, sounding as if he would if he had a break from the rehearsals.

Ferelith lightened the tension and brought the topic back to their dinner. 'Wrae recommends your raspberry cheesecake. We'll have two portions.'

'Coming right up.' Lochlen smiled and went through to the kitchen.

'I'll leave you, again, to enjoy your dinner,' Mor said with a smile, and went back over to join Creag and Torra. Creag was eating his risotto.

'Wrae says she'll put the red waistcoat aside for you,' Mor told Creag, sitting down to finish his dinner.

'I'll drop by their shop and try the waistcoat on, and if it fits, I'll wear it for the show,' said Creag.

'Ferelith plans to start work on a red version of your pink dress,' Mor said to Torra.

'Could you ask her to add plenty of sparkle to the bodice.' Torra tried to encourage Mor to go back over to tell Ferelith this.

'No, I've interrupted their dinner enough this evening.' Mor refused to be persuaded.

Torra sighed wearily. 'Then send her a message, or I'll go over and tell her. It could cause more work for her if she starts making the dress without knowing it needs adequate sparkle.'

To save Ferelith having to rework the dress, Mor sent her a message.

Would you please add plenty of sparkle to the bodice of Torra's dress. Thank you.

Ferelith and Wrae were enjoying the raspberry cheesecake when Ferelith saw the message pop up on her phone. 'It's from Mor,' she said to Wrae. She read it aloud, and then looked over at him and nodded.

He smiled back at her. Then he sent another message.

I loved hearing you play the piano. Will you play again tonight?

Ferelith read the message to Wrae.

'Are you going to play again?' Wrae said to her.

'No, the eatery is too busy. It would look like I was trying to grandstand.' Ferelith shook off the uncomfortable thought of this. It had felt easier playing to a few strangers earlier.

'I'm sure no one would think that,' said Wrae. 'I'd like to hear you play another sonata or a rhapsody.'

'I will, but not tonight, another time.'

Wrae smiled that she understood, and continued to eat her cheesecake.

Glancing over at Mor, Ferelith shook her head slowly without drawing anyone else's attention.

Mor smiled gently, and then signalled to the staff that he wanted to settle the bill before leaving. The three dancers didn't want any pudding, preferring a lighter dinner as they had the dance rehearsal later.

'I hope you enjoyed your meal, and we'll see you again,' Lochlen said to Mor, taking the payment.

'I did, and I'll certainly be back,' Mor assured him, lightening any previous tension that had existed between them.

'I think Mor and the others are leaving,' Wrae remarked.

Ferelith watched them start to head for the door, but a table of four women recognised Mor and waylaid him on his way out. Creag and Torra hung back while Mor obliged the ladies by having his photo taken with each of them.

'I keep forgetting how popular Mor is,' said Wrae.

Ferelith sounded wistful. 'So do I.'

'Creag doesn't seem put out that he's not being fawned over,' Wrae observed.

'Neither does Torra. Though Creag appears to be paying plenty of attention to her.'

Wrae viewed them carefully. 'I wonder if they're dating?'

'I don't think so,' said Ferelith. 'Torra doesn't look interested in Creag.'

Wrae agreed.

Mor finally extricated himself from the fans, and left the eatery to drive up to the dance studio with Torra and Creag.

Wrae read the poster advertising the ceilidh dance party night. 'Should we go to the ceilidh night?'

'Yes, if we're not working late on the show's costumes. But there's only one problem.'

Wrae frowned. 'What's that?'

'We've got nothing to wear.'

Wrae played along with the joke. 'We'll just have to rummage through all our wardrobes full of dresses.'

They laughed and chatted as they finished their dinner.

The lights from the window at the front entrance of the dance studio shone out into the evening, casting a glow on to the thoroughfare.

After parking the car nearby, Mor walked with Torra and Creag towards the entrance and went inside. The small reception was quite busy, and they went by and down the narrow corridor that separated the dance room where they were due to rehearse, and the stage room.

Mor and the other dancers changed into their dancewear at the studio. The dance room was brightly lit, and the dancers did their warm–up exercises, including using the ballet barre for stretching, ready to start the rehearsals. He'd booked the room for two hours, and set up his music to begin.

The choreography began with all eight of them dancing individually, then they partnered up to practise the lifts that Mor had planned for the new choreography.

Torra was partnered with Mor, while the others teamed up with their respective partners.

The twilight sun cast a burnished glow over the city as Ferelith and Wrae emerged from the eatery.

Lochlen walked them out. 'I hope to see you at the opening ceilidh dance night soon.'

'We'll do our best to attend,' Wrae promised him.

'It'll be a fun night,' he assured them. 'I'm wearing my kilt for the occasion, but just wear your gladrags and shoes you can dance in.'

'We will,' Ferelith chimed–in.

'And remember,' Lochlen added, 'come in and play the piano when you have the notion. You sounded great. I'd never have known you were out of practise, so practise on my piano.'

'I really should get a piano of my own,' said Ferelith. Though they were so expensive, and she didn't want to make a dent in their shop's profits to pay for a new piano, presumably to be kept at their cottage. Perhaps further down the line.

Lochlen looked thoughtful. 'Would you consider a pre–loved piano? An older piano that's still got plenty of tune in it.'

'I would,' said Ferelith, while thinking that classic pianos cost a fair bit too.

Wrae nodded, wondering if Lochlen had something in mind.

He did. 'I've been offered a few pianos for the eatery, at bargain prices. Often folk are just looking for someone to take the piano off their hands. Not many people want to scrap their pianos, especially if they were filled with fond memories of how they were played in their heyday.' Lochlen checked his phone. 'I've got their contact numbers here. I didn't take them up on their offers. One piano is enough for the eatery.'

He showed them a few of the messages, some of them just wanting a beloved piano taken away for free, or a token amount to have it picked up and delivered elsewhere.

The messages included pictures of the pianos, and they took a moment to scroll through the offers.

Ferelith saw a beautiful bargain. 'Oh, look at this gorgeous upright piano. It's like the one I first learned to play. Only this one is pink.'

Lochlen read the message accompanying it. 'Good home wanted for our old piano, preferably at the eatery where it'll be played. We're moving and can't take it with us. Free if you pay for the uplift and delivery.'

Wrae nodded at Ferelith. 'It's a lovely piano.'

Ferelith's eyes lit up with enthusiasm. 'We could make room for it at the cottage.' Then she reconsidered. 'Or at the shop. As it's an upright piano, it could fit into the gap beside the haberdashery.'

'A fancy enticement for those from the theatre to play while they're in for their fittings,' said Wrae.

'Do you want me to give them a call, see if it's still available?' Lochlen offered.

Ferelith and Wrae nodded and smiled as Lochlen made the call.

The exertion of the lifts showed in their dancing, reflected in the mirrored wall at the dance studio.

'Ease into the lifts,' Mor advised, demonstrating a different technique rather than the need for brute strength. 'Use the momentum of each movement.'

They ran through the routine again, seeing the improvement in the lifts.

'That's a lot better,' Mor told them. 'Now let's try it again with the music.'

Torra had danced with Mor in the past, and been his partner on dance tours. They were used to the ebb and flow of the lifts, where the power blended with their expert techniques.

'Take a break,' Mor said finally.

They went to the side and sat down to take a sip from their bottled water.

Mor joined them, standing, giving them more encouragement. 'I know I've raised the bar with this choreography, but I think it'll elevate the show to a spectacular level.'

They all agreed.

'I want to give audiences one of the most entertaining shows we're capable of,' said Creag.

After the short break, Mor and Creag teamed up with Torra, as did the other two male dancers, and one of the female dancers, ready to perform trio lifts. The other two female dancers stepped to the side, ready to take their turn at being lifted by the men in the three–person dance lifts.

Mor and Creag started first, facing the mirror. Torra approached from behind, dipping under the archway of their arms, and then they lifted her high above their shoulders, supporting her while she performed various positions in the air. Her ballet background came to the fore, and she looked like she was dancing in the air, making something difficult look smooth, elegant and effortless.

When they finished and placed her safely down on the floor again, Mor smiled and acknowledged her ability. 'One of the hardest things to do in dance is to make something hard look easy. And you just did that beautifully.'

Torra smiled, pleased that the lifts were working well.

The next trio then performed a variation on this, again receiving praise from Mor and the others.

Lochlen continued the phone call, securing the piano for Ferelith and Wrae. 'Their costume design shop is near the eatery. I'll forward the directions,' Lochlen told the seller. 'Tomorrow afternoon?' He glanced at them, and they nodded. 'Yes, that would be fine. They intend to put the piano in the shop. Ferelith is a classical pianist. She understands that the piano has been kept in tune, but will require retuning after being moved around during the delivery. Your piano is going to an appreciative home.'

The call finished on a cheery note. Lochlen smiled at Ferelith and Wrae. 'Well, that's it all sorted out.'

'We can't thank you enough,' Wrae said to Lochlen, thinking what a warm and kind smile he had standing there outside the eatery in the glow of the evening.

One of the catering staff came to the door and beckoned him in, needing his help in the kitchen.

'I'll be right there,' Lochlen confirmed, and then concluded his chat with Ferelith and Wrae. 'I'm sure I'll hear all about your new piano soon,' he said, encouraging their connection to continue.

'You certainly will,' Ferelith assured him.

'Perhaps you'd like to pop up to our shop one day,' Wrae added. 'We'll let you see the costumes and the piano. And have a cup of tea with us.'

'I'd like that. I'll bring cake.' Smiling at them, Lochlen then hurried into the eatery.

'Well, that was an unexpected bonus of having dinner here,' said Ferelith as they walked away.

'It was.' Wrae looked up at the sky as the amber glow gave way to the deep lilac and purple tones of the approaching night.

'I'm so excited about us having a piano in the shop.' Ferelith beamed with joy. 'We'll add a clip or two of you playing to our website.' Wrae pictured it would add an entertaining aspect to their costume business.

Ferelith viewed the pictures of the piano on her phone. 'It's so like the first piano I played, only in pink. And the upright design won't take up too much room in the shop.'

'We'll make it fit nicely,' Wrae assured her.

It was only a short walk to their shop, and the exterior lanterns were lit, providing a welcoming glow as they arrived.

Wrae unlocked the door and switched the lights on as they stepped inside. The door locked behind them, providing a bolthole where they could work uninterrupted on the costumes.

The first thing that Wrae did was unhook the red waistcoat from the spare rail and put it on the rail with the other costumes for the show.

Looking at the selection of red fabrics on the shelves, Ferelith lifted down a bolt of ruby red chiffon, one of sparkling scarlet tulle, and red stretch jersey.

The fabrics were arranged on the shelves according to colour, not by fabric type. This enabled them to see the colours clearly, comparing the tones from light to dark hues. Generally, each costume didn't have a wide mix of colours, but they were often made from a mix of fabrics, especially the dresses, using combinations such as rich velvet, brocade and satin, with light chiffon, organza and tulle.

She put the bolts down on the long cutting table and set about measuring the required lengths for Torra's dress, referencing the exact details from her folder of patterns.

Once she'd cut the lengths, she laid the paper pattern pieces on the fabrics, pinned them in place, and then cut each piece to size. They were now ready to be constructed and machine stitched together, starting with the bodice. The darts on the front and back of the bodice, that created the fitted shape, were tacked and machined first. Then the seams were sewn together.

While Ferelith had her measuring tape out, she checked the size given for the piano and went over to the haberdashery area where she planned to put it.

Wrae machine stitched the hem of the blue ballgown, and they chatted while they worked.

'The piano will fit nicely beside the haberdashery,' Ferelith confirmed.

'I think it'll add interest to the shop,' said Wrae. 'And you'll be able to practise again, though from your playing tonight, no one would guess that you hadn't played for so long.'

'I did enjoy playing it, but it'll be great to have a piano here where I won't feel I'm putting on a show.' She checked the positioning for the piano. 'We won't put it right up against the wall. It needs to sit out a wee bit, so that the sound can resonate. But it's a great type of upright, and we'll get it tuned after it arrives.'

'I noticed there was a baby grand piano offered to Lochlen too. Would you ever want one of those? A pre–loved one.'

'Maybe, but there would be no room for it in the shop. The upright fits neatly. Though I suppose I might get a baby grand bargain for the cottage and play at home. But not yet, further down the line.'

'You never know what Santa will bring you for Christmas,' Wrae hinted.

Ferelith laughed. 'I'd better stay on Santa's nice list.'

'And I'd better start stashing plenty of wrapping paper.'

Giggling, they continued chatting, and the conversation came round to Lochlen and inviting him to the shop.

'I know Lochlen told us he'd bring cake,' said Ferelith, 'but I think we should buy him cake so he can have something different from what's on his eatery menu.'

'Victoria sponge for afternoon tea?' Wrae suggested.

'No, he's got that on his menu, and chocolate cake, lemon drizzle and Dundee cake.'

'We'll need to come up with something tasty but different.'

'How about yum yums?' Ferelith said playfully.

Wrae laughed, and amid the chatter and smiles, they continued to work on their dressmaking.

CHAPTER FIVE

Upbeat music played while Mor and the dancers practised an energetic routine for the show. They'd honed the tango–style choreography, and worked on the lifts for a couple of the other routines. Overall, it had been a successful and energetic evening of dance practise.

'Well done, everyone,' Mor said, finally bringing the rehearsal night to a close.

They all got ready to leave and head home.

Mor was the last to leave, but eventually picked up his training bag, flicked the dance room lights off, and headed out into the night.

During the drive home through the heart of Edinburgh to where he lived in a detached house set within a garden in a leafy area of the city, he thought about Ferelith.

He pictured her smiling at him in the costume shop the first time they'd met, scolding him at the photo–shoot when he jumped into the air for an action shot and almost kicked one of the photographer's lights, and playing the piano at the eatery. Everything about her impressed and intrigued him.

Even during the night's dance rehearsal he found his mind drifting to Ferelith, wondering when he'd see her again, while knowing they were going to be in regular contact as she was making the show's costumes.

As he pulled up outside the front door of his house, the two–storey private property was in darkness. No welcoming glow of lights in the windows, or someone like Ferelith to come home to. He was of an age now when thoughts of settling down had replaced those of wanting to be fancy free and just live for his dancing and all the fun of a carefree lifestyle that went with it. The shine of such a life had been somewhat dulled recently. Now the thought of finding the woman of his dreams, settling down and building a life with her outshone everything.

Be careful, he warned himself as he went inside the silent house, and turned the lights on. Don't fall in love with Ferelith.

After showering and changing into silk pyjama bottoms, he padded through to the well–equipped kitchen, made himself a cup of tea, and took it through to the living room. The decor was in light, neutral shades with a mix of modern vintage furnishings. He sat down at the classic vintage bureau that he used as a desk.

He switched on his laptop and checked for messages, quickly answering those that needed his attention. Then he lifted one of his notebooks from a dookit in the bureau, and a pencil, and began to sketch the lifts that had been added to the show's choreography. He started a new notebook for every show he performed in, and this one was special because it was the first theatre show he'd headlined.

His drawings, by his own realistic assessment, were no match for the artistic illustrations that Ferelith and Wrae could create. But they were fine enough to help him record the choreography.

Several new costumes in various stages of being finished hung on a rail in the costume shop.

Ferelith was the last to turn off her sewing machine. Then she picked up her bag, ready to leave.

Wrae turned the shop lights off, and they stepped outside, and she locked the door.

The drive home to the cottage on the outskirts of the city was a relatively short one. A lantern lit the front door and the garden. The grass and flowers had become slightly overgrown, but Ferelith and Wrae intended tackling the garden together soon and getting it tamed. Tonight, the flowers, especially the night–scented stock, filled the air with a heady fragrance.

Wrae unlocked the door and they went inside and flicked the hall light on. It was late and they started to get ready for bed, heading into their respective bedrooms.

They'd had a cup of tea at the shop, so all they needed to do was get changed for bed and get some sleep. Another busy day lay ahead, including the arrival of the pre–loved piano.

The delivery was confirmed to be early in the afternoon, and they'd booked a piano tuner for the late afternoon, planning to have the piano tuned the same day.

By the glow of a couple of table lamps, Ferelith wandered through to the living room. It was traditionally furnished, as were all the rooms in the cottage. The living room was the ideal combination of having light and airy decor with glass patio doors opening out on to the back garden, and a cosy atmosphere. The fire was unlit, but gave a feeling of warmth even though the recent warm, sunny days, made it unnecessary. The main benefit of the fire would come during the colder months when they could sit by the fireside and sew and knit, or do whatever craft they cared for.

Ferelith mentally planned where a baby grand piano could go, if they ever bought a bargain one, giving it a welcoming home. She decided it would fit quite well over in the far corner at the patio area, and pictured herself sitting playing.

'I'm going to flop into bed,' Wrae called through to her.

'I'll do the same in a minute. Goodnight, Wrae.'

'Goodnight. Remember, it's an early start in the morning.'

Ferelith took the subtle hint that she shouldn't linger for too long before going to bed. And she didn't. She glanced around the room, noticing how many dressers and chests of drawers were filled with fabric and items they'd made, were in the process of making, or pipedream projects.

Bundles of pre–cut fabrics were stacked on a dresser beside the table where Ferelith's sewing machine was set up. Wrae's machine was over at the front window where she had a view of the pretty cottage garden.

As a fashion designer, and theatre costume designer, Ferelith loved the living room, a cosy hub where she could create her designs and sew. She loved the cottage and the garden, and felt fortunate to live there.

Turning the lamps off, she went through to bed, illuminated by the night glow shining through her bedroom window. There was a handmade quilt on her bed, sewn by her grandmother, and she got into bed and snuggled down for the night. The room had two large wardrobes and one smaller one. All of them were filled with costumes, clothes, fashions and falderals she refused to part with. Somewhere in one of the wardrobes were the clothes she wore for working in the shop, mainly items she'd sewn herself.

Lying there, she gazed out the window, seeing a scattering of stars glittering in the sky. And she thought about her day, particularly the parts where she was with Mor, and fell asleep picturing how easily he'd become part of her busy schedule.

The piano arrived on time, and the piano tuner made short work of tuning it. The piano had been well-maintained and required little adjustments. When he left, Ferelith stood back and admired the piano that was now due to be part of their shop.

It had come with a height-adjustable stool that contained a storage compartment when the lid of the stool was opened.

'Oh, look!' Ferelith exclaimed when she opened the lid of the stool and saw what was inside it. 'Music sheets.'

Wrae sat working at her sewing machine and looked over. 'What type of songs?'

Ferelith scanned the pages and smiled. 'Classics. A concerto, sonata, rhapsody, and popular songs.'

'Play something,' Wrae encouraged her.

'I should be working on the costumes.'

'Come on, a song to celebrate that we've got a piano in the shop.'

Ferelith took no further persuasion. She set up the sheet music for a rhapsody she loved, stored the other sheets inside the seat, put the padded lid down and sat ready to play.

The beautiful sound of the rhapsody resonated in the air, and Wrae smiled across at her sister, feeling as if they'd stepped back into the past when Ferelith considered a career in musical theatre.

Wrae hand–stitched sequins on to the bodice of the blue ballgown while listening to the song.

Ferelith felt the piano respond to her playing, and by the end of the rhapsody she was convinced that it was the perfect shop piano for her. And for Wrae, who enjoyed listening to the music.

Leaving the sheet music set up, Ferelith made them afternoon tea, and served it with two empire biscuits — shortbread biscuits sandwiched together with raspberry jam and topped with white icing and a glacé cherry. The sweet treat tasted delicious with their mugs of tea.

They were still having their afternoon tea when the buzzer sounded. Wrae looked surprised when she checked the monitor. 'It's Lochlen.' She barely recognised him at first as he wasn't wearing his chef whites. He wore dark trousers and a white shirt. She hurried to let him in, wondering if there was something wrong.

'I wondered if the piano arrived safely?' Lochlen said as Wrae welcomed him in.

'Yes, come in and take a peek. We were just having tea. Would you like a cup?' Wrae offered.

'Thanks,' he said, taking in the shop and the piano tucked over at the haberdashery area.

Wrae popped through to the kitchen to make him a tea while Ferelith showed him the piano. 'I've had it tuned, but it was well–kept and sounds beautiful. Such a great tone and a joy to play. Want to try it? You mentioned that you could play the piano.'

Lochlen smiled. 'I'm not very good. Nowhere near your ability.'

'Sit down and have a go.'

He sat down and took a deep breath, ready to play an easy tune, but then he noticed the sheet music propped up on the piano — and laughed. 'Were you playing this rhapsody?'

'It was inside the seat with various other music sheets.'

'My confidence just took a dive,' he said lightly.

'Nonsense, play anything,' she encouraged him.

'Okay, here goes...' he began to play a popular song, and surprised himself that his playing sounded not too bad.

Wrae came through with the tea tray. She'd made him a mug of tea, and put a yum yum on a plate for him. Ferelith had bought two empire biscuits and two yum yums from the bakery earlier.

'I like that song,' Wrae told him, putting the tray down on a table. 'You play it very well.'

'The lovely tone of this piano makes me sound so much better than I actually am,' he said.

'Nope,' Ferelith told him firmly. 'You can play just fine.'

Bolstered by their comments, Lochlen continued to play, but the buzzer sounded, and Wrae let Mor in.

Lochlen was still playing, and didn't notice it was Mor arriving.

'Apologies for interrupting,' said Mor, taken aback when he saw Lochlen playing a piano in the shop. 'Is this new? I don't remember seeing it.' He was sure he would've noticed a piano, but then again, he was so eager to get his costume adjusted for the photo–shoot, and interested in meeting Ferelith, perhaps he'd overlooked it.

Lochlen glanced round at him, gave him an acknowledging nod, and then continued playing.

'It's a pre–loved piano.' Ferelith summarised what had happened. 'A great bargain, basically a button buy. The owner wanted to sell it to someone who would appreciate it rather than discard it.'

'It has certainly found an appreciative new owner,' said Mor.

Lochlen finished playing and stood up. 'It fits in well with the shop.' He helped himself to the tea and the yum yum. 'This is delicious,' he mumbled. 'I must make these for the new menu.'

'Would you like a cup of tea?' Wrae said to Mor. 'I've just made a fresh pot.'

Mor's first inclination was to refuse, but then he heard himself reply, 'Yes, thank you.'

Wrae popped through to the kitchen, made a mug of tea for Mor, and put the last yum yum on a plate for him.

Mor accepted the tea and the yum yum. And for a moment, the two men were quiet as they ate the sticky iced treats and drank their tea.

Ferelith opened the lid of the piano seat and showed them the sheet music. 'There are some wonderful songs that were tucked into the seat.'

'Will you play for us?' Lochlen said to Ferelith.

Wrae nodded to her, hoping she would.

Sitting down, Ferelith propped up the music for another rhapsody, a romantic song that she used to enjoy playing, but hadn't done so in years. And yet, she was eager to give it a go.

'Let me film it.' Wrae got her phone ready. 'We'll put it on the shop's website. A news post, something of interest.'

'No pressure to get it right,' Ferelith joked.

'None at all,' Wrae said, joining in the fun. 'Just play really well and don't make any mistakes.'

Ferelith laughed, and as the mood lightened, she began to play the romantic rhapsody.

CHAPTER SIX

'That was beautifully played,' Mor said to Ferelith as she finished playing part of the rhapsody in the costume shop.

She stood up, and went over to take a sip of her tea. 'It's a beautiful piano.'

'We're pleased to give it a good home,' said Wrae.

'Do you play?' Lochlen said to Wrae.

'No, not at all. I don't have a talent for it, but I do enjoy listening,' Wrae explained. She viewed the piano and smiled. 'I'm sure it'll be a talking point for our clients when they come in for their fittings. Perhaps some of them might give us a tune, as many of them work in theatre and dance.'

'And they will be welcome to do so,' Ferelith confirmed with a smile.

'I confess, I didn't even know your shop was here until recently,' said Lochlen.

'We're well–hidden in our wee niche,' said Wrae.

'There's something cosy about being tucked away just off the main thoroughfare,' Ferelith added. 'Hidden almost in plain sight.'

'Most people contact us via our website,' said Wrae.

'Was there something you needed?' Ferelith said to Mor as he finished his tea.

'I was talking to my show director about the costumes, and we wondered if we could have flashes of red added to the costume colour theme?' Mor told her. 'We were thinking of things like a red tie or handkerchief. I could buy these items, but I thought I'd mention this to you and Wrae as you have such a great selection of fabric and perhaps you could make them to match the costumes.'

'We've made ties and hankies for costumes before,' said Wrae.

Ferelith went over to the range of red fabrics on a shelf. 'We have three types of red silk, in varying weights, that would work well.'

Sensing they were going to talk about business, and needed to get on with his own, Lochlen made a move to leave.

'Thank you for the tea and the yum yum, and for letting me play the piano,' Lochlen said to Wrae and Ferelith. 'I'd better get back to the eatery to start getting the dinners sorted.'

Wrae got ready to walk him out.

'Remember, the ceilidh dance party is on tomorrow night at the eatery,' Lochlen reminded them, including Mor in his invitation.

'We'll be there,' Wrae confirmed.

Ferelith saw no reason why they wouldn't be able to go along, and nodded and smiled.

'I have rehearsals tomorrow night at the dance studio,' Mor told Lochlen.

'This is the start of the ceilidh nights, so come along to another one when you're free,' Lochlen said to him.

'I certainly will,' Mor confirmed.

Wrae saw Lochlen out while Ferelith showed Mor the selection of red fabrics. She lifted down one of the bolts. 'We used this silk fabric to make your red shirt.

The fabric would make up nicely into hankies to tuck into the pockets of your jackets.' She let him feel the fabric.

Mor felt the silky fabric, and nodded, approving her idea.

'I'll cut a few pieces and hem the edges,' she said, putting the bolt down on the cutting table. 'The average size of a handkerchief is eight to twelve inches. I'll cut the larger size. It'll give you more to drape from the pockets, add a bit of flamboyance and colour coordinate with the costumes.'

'Will you make the ties with the same fabric to match?' said Mor.

'No, I'll use a heavier silk or satin.' She pulled down another two bolts of fabric to show him the weight, texture and colour.

Mor stepped forward to give her a hand to lift the bolts down from the shelf.

Feeling him so close, her heart reacted again, fluttering from being near to this handsome man.

Stop it, she scolded herself, glad of his help to lift the fairly heavy bolts of fabric down and put them on the table.

'These are heavier than I imagined,' he remarked, even though he lifted them with ease.

'The quality of the satin shows in the weight of it,' she said, unrolling it on the cutting table to show him the smoothness and rich red colour under the lights. 'Ties require a wee bit of work, but I've made them in the past, so has Wrae. We can check the costume list and see how many we need for the show.' She put the satin aside and concentrated on the silk for the hankies.

'You choose the fabrics with such ease. I wouldn't know where to start,' he admitted. 'Though I do have an interest in well–designed clothes.'

'I've always enjoyed working with fabric. This silk is one we order regularly for our stock. The density of the colour is ideal for theatre costumes.' She gestured to other fabrics on the shelf, a red polka and a red stripe design. 'These are lovely fabrics, but for something small, like a handkerchief, a plain tone is better as the audience can see it clearly under the stage lighting. In real life, they'd be nice, but not for the shows.'

'So many things have to be taken into consideration that I wouldn't have thought about,' he said.

'The smallest details won't show on stage during a performance. But often the actors or dancers have photographs taken, close–ups, to promote the shows, or at your meet and greets prior to or after the show when people have the chance to be photographed with you. The costumes have to be able to look great for both occasions.'

'Wearing wonderful costumes enhances my performance when dancing.'

'And it's important that you feel comfortable wearing it, and that it doesn't restrict your movements.'

'I imagine your past dance experience helps you step into the dancers' shoes when creating your designs.'

'It does. And Wrae took dance lessons when she was a girl, so we're both familiar enough with dancing to ensure the designs work when worn.'

Wrae came back in from chatting to Lochlen at the door. 'Lochlen says he's definitely wearing his kilt for the ceilidh dancing, so although we can wear what we want, I thought we could add tartan ribbon to our dresses.' She went over to the haberdashery where the selection of ribbons included silk tartan ribbon in three different colours. 'We can add flashes and tartan trims.'

'I think I'll wear the red wrap dress I made. You know the one,' said Ferelith.

'It would be lovely.' Wrae selected a roll of tartan ribbon in red tones from the display. 'This would work with it.'

'Ideal,' Ferelith confirmed. 'I'll add a trim of ribbon around the neckline.'

'I wish I could've joined in the ceilidh,' said Mor. 'There are ceilidh dance moves in the show's choreography.'

'Another night for sure,' Ferelith said to him with a smile.

'I'll wear one of my kilts.'

'You have more than one?' said Ferelith.

'I've got two. I love a good ceilidh.'

Ferelith continued to chat to Mor while cutting the fabric for the hankies. She lifted one of their see–through acrylic templates. They had various template sheets for cutting standard–size pieces of fabric that they used on a regular basis. The twelve–inch square template was well–used for their designs.

Mor watched, interested to see what she did with it.

'This saves time and helps with accuracy when cutting pattern pieces,' Ferelith explained. The silk fabric was unrolled on the cutting table. She handed him the template and a piece of tailors chalk to mark the fine lines around the edges of it. 'Would you like to try measuring and cutting one?'

He was more eager to try than she'd anticipated. 'What do I do first?' he said, holding the chalk and the template.

'Place the template down on the fabric. You'll noticed that the silk has a front and a back. You can tell the front of the fabric by the extra sheen. Put the template down on the back of the fabric because that's where the chalk marks go.'

Mor placed the template on the silk, right on the edge, thinking this would give him a straight edge on one side.

'Avoid the selvedge edge of the fabric,' said Ferelith, moving the template in a bit. 'The selvedge is to stop the silk from fraying, but we want all the edges of the hankie to be cut from the silk without the selvedge.'

Her hand brushed against his, and caused a spark between them. They both noticed it. Rather than pretend it hadn't happened, she accounted for it. 'There must be static from the silk.'

He agreed, while disbelieving this. The spark was from the deep attraction he felt for her, he was sure, though less sure if she felt the same.

Mor lined the template up, avoiding the selvedge, and under Ferelith's instruction, drew a line around the square using the tailors chalk. He looked pleased with himself that he hadn't messed it up as he lifted the template off to reveal a neatly–marked square.

'Well done,' she said. 'Now you have two choices. You can use a rotary cutter to cut the fabric, or a pair of scissors.' The scissors were professional dressmaking scissors.

Various types of scissors hung on a rack. The tailoring scissors they had tended to be heavier, made for heavy–duty cutting through thicker fabric for suiting, or denim and brocade. The dressmaking scissors were designed for precision cutting of lighter, delicate fabrics, that they often used for their dress pattern cutting, trimming seams and detailed work. They also had pinking shears, and embroidery scissors.

Before he could choose, the buzzer sounded and the door opened and in walked Efie, carrying bags of dresses she'd added sequins to. 'It's just me, girls,' she announced before stopping and beaming a bright smile when she saw Mor. 'Oh, it's yourself!'

'Hello, Efie,' he said, impressing her by remembering her name.

Efie smiled playfully. 'Ah, I see the girls have got you working, training you as their new apprentice.' She was so taken with him, she didn't notice the piano until later.

'I'm learning to cut a silk handkerchief.' He held up the rotary cutter in one hand and the gleaming dressmaking scissors in the other. 'Not sure what to use.'

'Have you ever used a rotary cutter?' said Efie.

'I never knew such accoutrements existed,' he admitted.

'Then use the scissors,' Efie advised him.

Ferelith and Wrae stood smiling, and watched as Mor took the scissors and began to cut along the chalk line.

None of them said a word, letting him concentrate, but flicked glances at each other, pleased that he was showing a hands–on interest in the costume making. It was only a hankie, but considering that Mor hadn't done any sewing, they were impressed by his willingness to give it a go.

Putting the scissors down on the table, he held up the perfectly–cut square of silk with a triumphant smile. 'I think I'll stick to dancing, but now I can say that I had a hand in making a tiny piece of the show's costumes.'

They smiled, genuinely pleased for him.

'Right, what's next?' he said, furthering the challenge.

'Can you use a sewing machine?' Ferelith said tentatively.

'Nope. You're looking at a man that can barely sew a button on his shirt. But I'm more than delighted to watch you do it. Then we'll swap skills, and I'll teach you all how to do fast–spinning pirouettes,' he said, teasing them.

Efie was the first to react. 'I'll just leave these bags here. I'm in a hurry to be somewhere else. Anywhere else.'

'I'm out of step with fast–spinning pirouettes,' said Wrae. 'But I'm sure Ferelith can do enough for all of us.'

Ferelith sunk her with a playful look. 'Pirouettes, perhaps, but fast–spinning ones?' She looked unsure.

On the spot, Mor performed the fastest pirouettes they'd seen up–close. Viewed on a stage maybe, but they felt the draft of his spins before he stopped without a wobble.

'There, nothing to it,' he joked.

Efie picked up the next bag of dresses that needed work. 'I'm away now. Nice seeing you again, Mor. And I'll hear all about the piano another time.' Giggling, she left them to get on with things and gave them a cheery wave.

Ferelith sat down at her sewing machine and threaded it up with red thread. A light shone down on the silk square and he watched her fold one edge of the fabric, turning it in twice so that the raw edges were enclosed in the hemming.

The whir of her sewing machine sounded as she fed the first side of the square through the machine. 'I turn in the corner like this,' she said. Then she continued machining the second edge.

'It's very neat, though I suppose you've had years of practise,' said Mor.

'I have, but the fun of sewing has never worn off. I love making things, even items like a silk square.'

When she came to the end of the fourth edge, she put the machine into reverse to secure the last few stitches. Then she cut the threads, leaving a long tail. 'I could snip it off, but it only takes a moment to thread a needle and slip the ends into the hem.' She did just that, and then cut the threads so that the ends disappeared into the hem, creating a lovely neat finish.

'There you go.' Ferelith handed it to him. 'Wear it for the show. The one you helped to make.'

He was delighted with this, folded it carefully and tucked it in his trouser pocket. 'Thank you.' His smile warmed her heart.

Wrae was now busy sewing one of the costumes, and he felt it was time to leave.

'I'll let you get on with your work.' He tapped his pocket. 'I'll be sure to wear this for the show.'

Ferelith walked him to the door and waved him off, feeling a tug at her heart watching him walk away in the glow of the fading sun.

Then she went inside and got on with her sewing. They'd had another busy day, and planned to work on into the early evening.

CHAPTER SEVEN

Wrae sat at her sewing machine, working on one of the costumes, finishing a hem. They'd worked all evening in the shop, and were due to tidy up and go home soon.

Ferelith used a fine–tip black pen to sketch a new dress design, creating an inked illustration of the style she had in mind. The artistic sketch showed the fluid lines of the dress, how it would look on a figure, the mid–length hem and detailed bodice.

Wrae finished machining and snipped the ends of the thread off. Easing the tension from her shoulders, she stood up, and hung the dress on one of the rails.

As she walked by, she stopped to look at Ferelith's illustration. 'I like the design of this dress. Glamorous, but suitable for dancing. There's lots of movement in the skirt.'

'We could work from our own leotard base pattern, but attach an illusion neckline and illusion sleeves.'

They often used sheer stretch fabrics to create necklines and sleeves that were then embellished with sparkle beads or sequins. The sheer fabric subtly secured the neckline of a low–cut bodice. And when the sparkle was added to the see–through fabric it created the illusion of it having been sprinkled on to the neck area and arms. This effect was particularly popular with their clients, and looked wonderful under stage lighting.

Wrae went over to their stock of fabrics and lifted down a bolt of sheer, stretch fabric that sparkled with gold glitter, and one with pink sparkles. 'These would look gorgeous.'

They had a wide range of colours in the sheer glittering fabrics that were used for the illusion designs too, and didn't need any sequins or sparkle added.

Ferelith came over to view the fabrics under the lights. 'We need four matching dresses for one of the opening routines, and four for the end of Act Two. I think we'll use the gold for the opening. And I'll make a variation in pink for another design.'

Wrae agreed, and they checked the dance show's costume list. 'The brief says they want lots of sparkle for the performances. And these would work perfectly.'

'I'll make a sample up in the morning and get it approved by Mor and his show director,' said Ferelith.

They started to tidy up. But as Wrae put the sheer fabric back on a shelf, she noticed an end of the roll piece of silk tartan fabric. 'Look, we've got a spare piece of silk tartan. It was tucked at the back of the shelf.' She pulled it down and unrolled what there was of it on the cutting table. 'I used this a while ago for making silk back waistcoats.'

'How much is left?'

Wrae removed the piece from the roll and laid it along the measurer that was on one edge of the table. 'About two and a half metres. The fabric is around a metre wide. We could make two tartan sashes to wear at the ceilidh. Cut the fabric lengthwise down the middle, trim it to size. Each piece would be like a long scarf.'

'They would be easy to make. Just hem the edges.'

'It would probably take less time than sewing tartan ribbon on to your dress neckline. We could wear the sashes with our dresses for the ceilidh,' said Wrae.

'Let's make them.'

Wrae smoothed out the fabric on the table and then cut two pieces lengthwise. She handed one of the long, rectangular pieces to Ferelith.

Sitting down at their sewing machines, they threaded them up to match the main red tones of the tartan, and then hemmed the edges of the fabric to create the sashes.

Their sewing machines whizzed along the edges, and they finished the hemming in less than ten minutes.

Wrae shook out her sash. 'This will look lovely. There are various ways we can wear the sashes, but I like mine draped over my right shoulder and across to my left hip.' She'd worn sashes before when attending ceilidh dances at Hogmanay parties.

'So do I.' Ferelith reached up to a box that had a selection of fancy costume clips. 'Secure the ends with one of these, instead of tying a knot, and clip the top to the shoulder of your dress, rather than wear a brooch to hold the sash in place.'

Wrae accepted the two clips, and put her sash on, securing it with the clips, and then danced around. 'I like this. It's light and it'll give us the wee touch of tartan we need for the ceilidh.'

They then continued to tidy up the shop.

Wrae checked their website for messages, and was surprised to see there were a few comments on the video clips she'd put up showing Ferelith playing the piano.

'We've had a great reaction to your piano playing,' Wrae told her.

Ferelith came over, read the comments and smiled.

'They love your playing, and like that we've got a piano in the shop,' said Wrae.

Chatting cheerfully about this, they then switched everything off, secured the shop and headed home.

Mor and the dancers finished their rehearsal at the dance studio and got ready to leave.

'We have rehearsals tomorrow night,' Mor reminded them, and then told them about Lochlen inviting him along to the ceilidh night at the eatery. 'I wondered, as we're including some ceilidh dance moves in our choreography, if you'd like to finish half an hour early tomorrow and head along to the eatery's ceilidh night.'

'I'm up for that,' Creag was the first to say.

The others were happy to go.

'It'll give us some practise dancing at the ceilidh,' Mor added.

'Is there a dress code?' said Torra.

'No, but I'm going to wear a kilt and a ghillie shirt,' Mor told her.

'I'll bring my kilt and a shirt along to rehearsals tomorrow night,' said Creag. 'I've got a kilt I wear to Hogmanay parties.'

The two other male dancers didn't have kilts, but agreed they'd turn up smartly dressed. The ladies planned to wear dresses.

Mor, Creag and Torra were the last ones to leave the dance studio and chatted about the silk handkerchief Mor had shown them he'd made.

'Are you thinking of having a side career in theatre costume design?' Creag joked with him.

'Nooo, Ferelith encouraged me, but I don't think I have a knack for sewing,' said Mor.

'You seem to be getting along well with Ferelith,' Torra remarked.

'There's no romance if that's what you're hinting at,' Mor told her.

Torra smiled at him.

'I'm not getting involved romantically with anyone,' Mor insisted. 'I'm concentrating on getting the show ready.'

Torra nodded. 'So am I. I've put romance on hold too. I'm far too busy with the dance rehearsals and costume fittings to even think about dating.'

Creag made a huge effort to hide his disappointment, but then was bolstered by the thought that at least Torra wasn't interested in dating anyone else. There was still a chance for him.

The three of them went their separate ways outside the studio.

Mor drove home, planning to relax and make himself an easy supper.

Arriving at the house, he parked the car, and took a moment to breathe in the fresh night air before heading inside and through to the kitchen.

His thoughts concentrated on the dance show, the choreography and all the aspects he had to attend to. And he thought about Ferelith playing the piano. Wrae had said she was going to put a video up on the shop's website. He made himself a cheese and tomato toastie and a mug of tea, and then went through to his desk in the living room.

While eating his tasty supper, he checked the shop's website on his laptop. And there was the clip of Ferelith playing the piano. His heart took a hit seeing her, looking sweet and lovely. Despite what he'd told Torra and Creag earlier, he couldn't help feeling attracted to Ferelith, but he again warned himself not to get involved romantically, not when he was right in the midst of such a busy schedule.

He drank his tea and replayed the clip again, enjoying the quality of her playing, and admiring her talent for music as well as costume design.

Ferelith wore her comfy pyjamas and slippers, and wandered through from the living room, hearing mild chaos from Wrae's bedroom.

Walking in, she saw Wrae rummaging through one of her wardrobes that was half full of dresses she'd made. The other half were piled on the bed where they'd been discarded in Wrae's effort to find a particular dress she wanted to wear to the ceilidh.

'Are you winning?' Ferelith said, sitting down on the only vacant edge of the bed.

Wrae wrestled another two dresses off a hanger, finding a third dress underneath. It wasn't the one she was looking for, so she layered the hanger back up with the trio of dresses and tossed it on to the top of the pile.

'Do you remember that lovely pale yellow dress I made last summer?'

'The one with the gorgeous silky fabric?'

'Yes, I can't find it anywhere, but it has to be here somewhere. I'd like to wear it tomorrow night. It's light and feels so nice. I don't know if Lochlen's opening ceilidh night will be busy or not, but it's bound to be warm, especially once we're all up jigging and whirling around the dance floor.'

'Do you think I should rethink wearing my red dress?'

'No, it's fairly light, and suits you so well.' She sighed wearily. 'I just would've liked to have worn the yellow dress.'

Ferelith smiled to herself as Wrae reached further into the wardrobe, almost disappearing into the depths of it. Beside her on the bed, she saw the yellow dress peek out from under the pile. Wrae must've thrown it there along with the others, not realising it was on the hanger.

'Here you go.' Ferelith held the dress up.

Wrae looked round and stared. 'Where did you find it? I've looked everywhere.'

'It was under the snowstorm of dresses on the bed.'

Wrae smiled and grabbed the dress, held it up and looked at herself in the wardrobe mirror. 'What do you think?'

'You'll look gorgeous in it. And the sash will go well with it too.'

Ferelith went through to her bedroom, dug out one of the tartan sashes from her bag, and brought it back through.

Wrae was now wearing the yellow dress, and gleefully put the sash on. Gazing at her reflection in the mirror, she smiled brightly. 'I love it!'

'You suit the design.'

'You should try your dress on,' Wrae encouraged her. 'In case it needs sorted.'

This seemed like a sensible idea, so Ferelith went back to her bedroom, found the red wrap dress, and put it on. When she added the sash, the design of the dress went up a few notches, and she hurried through to show Wrae.

'Oh, yes, that's an eye–catching look for you,' Wrae confirmed.

Standing side by side, looking at themselves in the full–length mirror, Ferelith felt a rush of excitement. 'We're ready for the ceilidh.'

Wrae's auburn hair was pinned up in a chignon, the style she'd worn all day. 'I'm going to wear my hair up for the dancing.'

Ferelith's fiery red hair was swept up in a ballet bun, as she often wore it for work. 'I think I'll wear mine up too. We've been to a few New Year ceilidh parties celebrating Hogmanay, and they can be quite energetic. Lochlen's party could be a wee bit wild.'

'It's a shame that Mor won't be there. Imagine seeing a dancer like him burling around the dance floor doing a reel or a jig,' said Wrae.

Ferelith nodded thoughtfully. 'It would've been fun to be on a dance floor with him. We're no match for his talents, but imagine dancing with him.'

'Mor told Lochlen he'd go another night, so we'll go too and wangle a dance,' Wrae suggested.

'Yes, though you're far better at Scottish Highland and ceilidh dancing than me.'

Wrae sighed and smiled. 'I used to love going to my dance lessons, though I've forgotten most of the things I learned.'

'That's nonsense. Whenever we're at any ceilidh, your Highland and Scottish country dancing skills shine through. Unless Mor trained likewise, you could be a match for his ability, maybe even a smidgen better.'

'Well, Mor won't be there tomorrow night, so we can relax and enjoy ourselves without competing with a pro like him.'

Ferelith nodded, and then went through to take off her dress. She hung it up on the outside of the wardrobe, along with the tartan sash, ready to take with her to the shop in the morning. They planned to head to the ceilidh night after finishing work at the shop.

'I checked the eatery's website,' said Wrae. 'Lochlen is laying on a tasty buffet for the dancing, so we won't even have to cook dinner before we pop along.'

'Handy.'

'The menu at the eatery is so tempting,' said Wrae.

'Are you including Lochlen?' Ferelith teased her.

'I admit that spending more time with him has made me appreciate how attractive he is. And he's fun to chat to. Plus he was very helpful suggesting the piano.'

'He was. I like Lochlen,' Ferelith admitted. 'Not in a romantic way, but as a friend.'

'It's handy to have a friend in business nearby,' said Wrae.

'Especially if he's as good looking as Lochlen.'

Wrae laughed, and then they continued to plan their day, and the ceilidh night fun.

CHAPTER EIGHT

Ferelith and Wrae were working at their sewing machines the next morning, making the costumes for the dance show, when Lochlen phoned the shop.

Ferelith took the call while Wrae continued her dressmaking, hand–stitching sequins on to the bodice of a ballgown.

'Morning, Lochlen,' Ferelith said brightly.

'I hope you and Wrae are still coming along to the ceilidh tonight,' he said.

'Yes, we're looking forward to it.'

'I wanted to ask you a favour, and it's okay if you don't want to do it,' he began.

'What's that?'

'I'm planning to film video clips of the ceilidh to put up on the eatery's website. Would you be willing to play the piano? Even for a couple of minutes, to show that customers are welcome to play it. You play so well.'

'Yes, I'd be happy to do that for you. What do you want me to play?'

'I'd leave that up to you.'

'I could play something with a Scottish theme as it's a ceilidh,' she suggested.

'That would be great.' He then offered to pay her for her time, but she brushed this aside.

'I'm glad to help,' Ferelith assured him.

'Thanks so much,' said Lochlen, and then let her get on with her work.

Ferelith told Wrae.

'I'd love to hear you play again. What song do you have in mind?'

'I've a couple that are popular.' She quickly sat down at the piano and played them. They were songs she'd played often and knew so well that she didn't need sheet music.

Wrae continued stitching the sequins on to the dress while she listened. 'I like them both. The second song is livelier, so people might be encouraged to get up and dance while you're playing,' said Wrae.

Ferelith hadn't thought about this. 'I'll play that song, keep the music lively. And save the other song in case I need it as back–up.' She played the songs again for practise.

Then she continued working on the illusion dress she'd designed, adding the sleeves using the sheer gold glitter fabric. She'd already attached the illusion neckline. Although this was supposed to be a sample dress, she'd made it so it could be used as one of the costumes with just a little more work added to it once it was approved.

Ferelith and Wrae continued to work right through until lunchtime, and then sat outside the front of the shop in the sunshine to eat their salad and coleslaw baguettes and drink their tea. They kept two folding chairs and a table for sitting outside. The flowers were thriving and the scent added to the relaxing atmosphere. Sitting out from under the canopy, they enjoyed the sunlight.

After lunch, they continued their costume design work until it was time to get ready for the ceilidh. They'd brought their dresses, sashes, shoes and other items to the shop, and got dressed there. Their shoes were made for dancing at ceilidh parties such as the New Year Hogmanay celebrations.

Before leaving to go along to the ceilidh, Ferelith practised playing the songs again on the piano in the shop.

The windows of the eatery were aglow in the evening light as Ferelith and Wrae approached the front entrance. Music filtered out as they went inside.

Lochlen, wearing his kilt, sporran and a white shirt and dark waistcoat, welcomed them in.

The eatery was already starting to get busy with people arriving for the fun night of ceilidh dancing and the delicious buffet that was set up along one wall in the function room. Meals were still being served in the restaurant area where the piano was located. No one was playing the piano. Not yet.

'You both look lovely,' Lochlen told them. 'Help yourself to the buffet.'

Ferelith looked over at the piano. 'When would you like me to play?'

'Whenever it suits you,' said Lochlen. 'I'm going to announce the start of the ceilidh dancing in a few minutes. I've organised one of the staff to take video clips throughout the evening. He knows to film you whenever you play.'

'I think I'll play now, before it gets any busier.' Ferelith headed over to the piano and sat down.

Wrae went with her and stood aside while Ferelith settled herself for a moment.

Lochlen spoke to the camera. 'To celebrate our ceilidh night, Ferelith, a theatre costume designer, is going to play for us. The piano is available for anyone to play when coming in for a meal in the restaurant or attending one of the functions.' Smiling, he stepped aside.

Ferelith began to play the piano.

The staff member recorded her performance.

Above the busy chatter, people stopped to listen, and hearing the lively song a number of them started to dance. Everyone was well–dressed for the party, with many of the men wearing kilts.

As Ferelith finished playing, Lochlen announced the official start of the ceilidh, standing on the small stage in the function room.

'Welcome to our ceilidh dance party night,' Lochlen said, smiling at everyone. 'I hope you enjoy the buffet, the music and a fun evening of ceilidh dancing.' He stepped down and then hurried away to ask Wrae and Ferelith to dance with him.

Clasping their hands, he led them through to the function room and they joined in the lively reel.

It was one of those reels where everyone danced with everyone else, whirling around the floor. The music was cheery and got people up to join in the dancing.

The ceilidh got off to a great start, and as the reel finished, everyone continued dancing to the following jig.

Finally taking a break from the dancing, Ferelith and Wrae went over to have something to eat and drink at the buffet. They hadn't eaten dinner, knowing they'd have something to eat during the ceilidh. Ferelith helped herself to a pastry filled with mashed potato and Scottish cheddar. Wrae opted for a slice of savoury lattice pie.

'Are you enjoying yourselves?' Lochlen came over to say to them.

'We certainly are,' Wrae confirmed.

'The food is delicious,' Ferelith told him.

Lochlen beamed a bright smile. 'I'm pleased you like it. I selected some of my favourite buffet dishes, particularly the pastries and pies. And make sure to indulge in a slice of chocolate cake and Victoria sponge. I baked them myself.'

'We will,' said Wrae.

Lochlen was then pulled into the dancing by a couple of the revellers, and Ferelith and Wrae continued to enjoy the buffet.

Mor and the dancers finished their rehearsals at the dance studio with another ceilidh dance routine.

'Well done again tonight,' Mor said to them, and then checked the time. 'We'd better get dressed for the ceilidh.'

Mor put on his kilt and sporran, and a white ghillie shirt. The neckline laced up the front, and he left the laces undone, exposing part of his chest. He wore cream wool, knee–length socks and ghillie brogues.

Creag's outfit consisted of a black ghillie shirt worn with a dark grey and black tartan kilt. The dramatic look suited him, and he thought he caught Torra giving him an admiring glance.

The two other male dancers wore tartan ties with their white shirts and dark trousers. It was enough to show that they'd dressed for the ceilidh.

Torra surprised them all by wearing a red tartan kilted skirt, short–sleeve white blouse and a red waistcoat. 'I wore this outfit for a show a couple of years ago and kept it in case I ever went to a ceilidh. The show had Scottish dance routines and I learned a few of the dances.'

'You suit it,' said Creag.

Mor agreed.

The other two ladies wore dresses and tartan bows on their necklines.

Packing up their things, they all drove down to the eatery.

Ferelith had been persuaded to play the piano again, and finished her rendition of the second Scottish song unaware that she was being watched by a man from across the room. He was in his thirties, and was with a small party of friends sitting at a table in the restaurant area.

A large reel had formed in the function room as a lively song came to an end with people smiling and catching their breath.

Mor, Creag, Torra and the other dancers walked in as the music started for another dance.

'Ah, good, we're not too late!' Mor shouted over the music, causing a number of faces to look round at him as he approached Lochlen. 'Can we join in?'

'Yes, come away in, Mor, and bring your friends,' Lochlen said, welcoming them through to the function room.

The ceilidh, that was already going well, suddenly had a burst of new energy with the happy arrival of the dance troupe.

Rather than keep to themselves, Mor and the other dancers spread out among the partygoers and mixed into the ceilidh reel.

Mor kept looking around, hoping to see Ferelith and Wrae.

Ferelith peered through to the function room. 'Mor has turned up!' she said to Wrae.

Peeking round, Wrae looked surprised. 'He's brought Torra, Creag and the others from the dance show with him!'

Ferelith's face lit up with excitement. 'Do you want to go through and join in?'

Wrae nodded and smiled, and they wound their way through the revelry.

Standing at the edge of the dance floor, they waited for the opportune moment to step in and began whirling around, taking part in the energetic dancing.

Mor brightened, seeing Ferelith, and they linked arms and held hands a few times as everyone danced with everyone else during the fast–moving reel.

'I didn't think you'd be here,' Ferelith said as he whirled her around.

'We're making it part of tonight's rehearsals,' Mor said, and then they were separated as the reel picked up pace.

Lochlen was eager to dance with Wrae, and used his experience to wangle his way over so that he was partnered with her for the remaining section of the dance.

Clasping her hands he whirled her around.

'No, Lochlen!' Wrae squealed and giggled. 'You're going too fast!'

'Don't worry, Wrae, I won't let you skite. You're safe in my arms.'

And in that moment, Wrae believed she was, and gave herself over to being spun and occasionally lifted off her feet by the capable Lochlen.

'I've had the fashion illustrations framed,' Mor managed to tell Ferelith as the song ended and another began. 'I've got them hanging on my wall at home, alongside the show's new poster. I'll give you a copy of the poster if you want.'

'Yes, I'd like one.'

For the next several dances there were extra cheers and laughter as various people got to dance with the professional dancers.

Ferelith danced with Creag and the other professionals, and with Lochlen who was skilled at ceilidh dancing and often led the dancing when others were unsure of the next sequence.

Daring dancing raised the bar for the following reel as the professional dancers took to the floor with their selected partners.

Mor clasped Ferelith's hand. 'Are you up for some fun?'

'Oh, yes,' said Ferelith, wondering what Mor had in mind.

'Face me, and as the introduction starts, clasp your hands around my shoulders,' he instructed.

'And then what?'

'Hold on!'

Ferelith laughed, and glanced over to see that Lochlen had encouraged Wrae to partner with him, and Torra was dancing with Creag. The other four dancers had partnered up themselves, and there was a sense of fun in the air as the music began.

Mor started to spin, whirling Ferelith around, lifting her feet slightly off the floor. The momentum made it feel like she was being twirled around, but held secure by Mor's strong arms.

She could barely do anything for squealing and giggling, not only from the sensation of being burled around by Mor, but also from seeing Wrae and Torra experiencing the same level of excitement.

The fun of the dance was enjoyed by those taking part, and by others standing around the edges of the floor clapping and cheering them on. The whole escapade lasted only a couple of minutes, and then everyone danced on, clasping hands with their partners and then linking arms as they skip–stepped around the floor.

The dance finished with cheers, laughter and applause, raising the fun level of the atmosphere.

And then Lochlen announced the next dance.

Lots of people stepped aside to get a refreshment and catch their breath, but there were some that got their second wind and were ready to dance. This included Mor and Ferelith, Lochlen and Wrae, and Creig and Torra.

Another lively dance got everyone cheering again, and when it finished, a particular dance was next on the schedule.

'Anyone up for a lively Highland dance?' Lochlen announced from the stage.

A handful of people stepped on to the floor, while the majority preferred to watch.

'I'm not experienced in Highland dancing,' Ferelith said to Mor. 'I know the popular ceilidh dances, but Highland dancing is different. I'd prefer to sit this one out.'

'Let's watch the fun,' Mor agreed.

Wrae looked over at Ferelith, wondering if she should take part.

Ferelith nodded encouragingly, knowing that Wrae was great at Highland dancing.

On the other side of the floor, Torra got ready to dance and beckoned Creag to join her.

'I'll give it a go,' Creag said to Torra. 'But I don't know many Highland dance moves.'

'Watch what I do, and drop out when you can't handle the tricky steps,' Torra advised. 'I'm not trained in Highland dancing, but I have danced this type of routine on stage, so I'd like to join in.'

Creag nodded, eager to try his best.

'Are you up for it?' Lochlen whispered to Wrae.

'I am. I did a bit of Highland dancing when I was a wee girl.' Wrae didn't mention the local contests where she'd won medals and a couple of trophies. These were for minor competitions, and she didn't want to overestimate her skills. She wasn't sure if she'd remember the steps. But seeing Ferelith nodding encouragement to her, she decided to let her hair down, just for tonight, and see how much of her past training and skills she'd retained.

As the music introduction played, those taking part lined up on the floor, taking a space to perform on their own. It was a solo routine, danced on the spot.

Wrae felt her heart soar with excitement, recognising the song, and the dance, one of her favourites from her past. She'd never been the highly competitive type, and when she'd taken part in contests when she was a girl, it had been for the love of the dancing, and the joy of the fun events.

Ferelith looked over at her sister, knowing what she'd been capable of in the past. *Come on, Wrae*, she thought, wanting her to shine, willing her to do well.

CHAPTER NINE

It finally came down to a lively dance–off between Torra and Wrae.

Torra's professional dance expertise and performance ability upped the challenge.

Wrae's technique was surer, and despite not having practised this particular Highland dance for a while, Wrae was able to keep up with the fast pace, and was precise in her steps. The steps included heel–and–toe combinations and back steps.

They were both in sync with the rhythm of the music. As a dancer, Torra's posture was excellent, and her core was strong.

But Wrae's posture, and her arm positions when she danced looked great. When Wrae raised her arms they were gracefully curved, palms facing in, finger positions elegant. Wrae's up springs and landings looked effortless even though the elevated techniques were difficult.

Torra was able to pick up the steps quickly, learning as she went along, and could then repeat the steps without further prompting. She was fit too, from all the dance training. Wrae was fit from hard work and a natural tendency to maintain a lithe and limber build. There were numerous jumps, leaps, and intricate footwork in the dance. Some of these had a balletic quality, and both Torra and Wrae moved with grace and poise.

The challenge reached a crescendo in time with the music, increasing in pace.

'Go, Wrae!' Ferelith shouted above the lively song, forgetting about decorum to encourage her sister.

Hearing Ferelith cheering her on, Wrae rose to the last part of the challenge that came down to fast and accurate footwork with her arms raised in high position.

Everyone was cheering both of them on, though Wrae heard Lochlen's voice encouraging her above the merry melee.

Despite Torra's excellent dance ability, Wrae was the clear winner.

Applause and cheers filled the room, and Lochlen came bounding over to Wrae, along with Ferelith, while Creag headed to bolster Torra. The whole dance was captured on video, though Lochlen didn't intend putting anything like this up without Wrae and Torra being happy for him to do this.

The music was set for the next song to play, a ceilidh waltz. While Lochlen invited Wrae over to the buffet for a refreshment after the energetic, but friendly dance–off, Mor held out his hand to Ferelith.

'Would you like to dance?'

'Yes,' she said, and let him lead her on to the floor where they joined other couples.

Taking Ferelith in hold, they began to waltz to the traditional music.

Feeling his gentle strength sweep her around, she tried to hide the effect he had on her. He was the most handsome man she'd ever danced with, and here she was, waltzing with him as if they were a couple.

And for a moment, she let herself feel what it would be like to be in a relationship with Mor. But every sensible thought fought against the wild urge to take a chance and let herself fall in love with him a little, perhaps a lot. It could never work she warned herself. His life was in the world of dance, never settled, always travelling, performing, and this wasn't the type of life that she wanted to fit into. She wouldn't fit in with Mor's world. Would she? If he was even interested in dating her. She could see nothing but compromises and broken promises, despite the love and passion such an involvement would offer.

'Look at Wrae and Torra,' Mor said, nudging Ferelith from her wayward thoughts.

She glanced over to where Wrae and Torra were standing at a quieter area of the function room. Wrae was showing Torra some of the steps from the Highland dance, sharing the techniques, and giving Torra ideas for the show's ceilidh routines.

Ferelith smiled, watching the two of them getting along, and then Creag joined them and practised too.

'I can see that I'll be adding new moves to the choreography,' Mor said to Ferelith.

She smiled. 'It was great seeing Wrae dance again.'

Mor then noticed Lochlen watching Wrae, admiring her while he was attending to the buffet.

'Lochlen really seems to like Wrae,' he remarked.

'She likes him too, but she's like me, neither of us is looking for romance at the moment.'

Mor hid the stab of disappointment her remark caused, and continued to waltz with her.

'I suppose you're concentrating on your theatre costume work,' said Mor.

'Yes, I'm busy enough with the designs and dressmaking without adding the complications of romance into the mix.'

'Romance doesn't have to be complicated surely. A couple can help bolster each other.'

'From my experience, romance tends to complicate everything.'

'Maybe you need new and better experiences,' he reasoned.

She was about to agree with him, when the song finished and another lively reel began.

'Shall we get something to drink from the buffet?' Mor suggested.

Ferelith was happy to do this, but as they were walking over to the buffet, the man who'd been watching her earlier approached them.

'I saw you play the piano,' the man said to her with a smile. 'And I hear that you're preparing for your new dance show,' he added to Mor. 'I'm a journalist for one of the papers based here in Edinburgh. I wondered if I could interview the two of you. I understand that you're designing the costumes for Mor's show,' he said to Ferelith.

She glanced at Mor to see his reaction to the journalist's request.

'Yes,' Mor agreed, seemingly used to being approached and happy to be featured in the press to promote his show.

The journalist told them what paper he was with, and that he'd like to include a mention of Lochlen's eatery, highlighting that the show's dancers had turned up for the ceilidh night.

There were a few angles he wanted to take with the story, and they discussed these while the party atmosphere swirled around them.

'Lochlen invited me along to the ceilidh night,' Mor explained to the journalist. 'We had dance rehearsals up at the new dance studio, but as we're including ceilidh choreography in the show, we came down to join in the real ceilidh dancing.'

'Will you be adding some of these moves into your choreography?' the journalist said to him.

'Definitely,' said Mor, and then they chatted about Wrae and Torra's dancing.

The journalist used his phone to record the interview. 'Wrae is your sister, and you both own the theatre costume design shop near here,' he said to Ferelith.

'That's right,' said Ferelith, giving him brief details of their business and the costumes they were making for the show.

Mor chipped–in about Ferelith coming along with him to the photo–shoot for the show's poster, and the journalist was eager to hear all the snippets of interest. He also took photos of them posing in a ceilidh waltz stance, and then together while Ferelith sat at the piano.

She told the journalist about the recent purchase for the shop.

'A pink piano!' the journalist exclaimed when he heard what was added to their shop. 'Could I pop round in the morning and take a picture of it, and an exclusive peek at some of the show's costumes?'

Ferelith agreed he could, and Mor was happy for the costumes to be featured in the editorial.

By now, Lochlen was involved in the interview, along with Wrae, Torra, Creag and the other dancers.

Before the journalist left, he interviewed Lochlen and took pictures of him in the eatery.

'I came for the ceilidh with some friends,' the journalist explained as he snapped the last few pictures. 'It's a night off, but then I saw Ferelith playing the piano and the show's dancers joining in the ceilidh and thought it would be a great story for our readers.'

After arranging to drop by the costume shop in the morning, the journalist finished the interview and went back to join his friends.

The evening was drawing to a close, and concluded with Lochlen announcing the last dance of the night — a romantic slow dance.

Mor partnered with Ferelith, and as the lights dimmed, creating a romantic atmosphere, he wrapped his arms around her waist, while she draped hers around his shoulders. Other couples filled the floor, including Torra and Creag and Lochlen and Wrae.

Mor gazed down at Ferelith. 'I think the interview will be interesting, and it'll promote your shop as well as the dance show.'

'Yes, it'll be great publicity, though I haven't been featured in the papers before, and never imagined it would be because I was playing the piano.'

'I'm sure people will be interested in your costume designs too.'

'Is the kilt you're wearing tonight the one you want me to add sparkle to?'

'No, I have my dance show kilt at home. I can drop it off in the morning at your shop,' he suggested.

'Do that. I'll get it sparkled up for you,' she said.

For the remainder of the slow dance, Mor held her close, and they moved to the romantic rhythm of the music, lit by the overhead twinkle lights. She felt the lean, strong contours of his muscles press against her as they danced.

Mor's strength was evident, and they finished the slow dance face–to–face. His lips were a tempting breath away from hers, and in that other world where she dared to dream of romance with a man like him, she would've given in to the temptation of his sensual lips.

Sensing the temptation strongly, Mor stepped back, while still holding her hand, and added a flourishing move, spinning her away from him, and nodding his thanks to her for the dance.

When he finally let go of her hand, she felt a pang of longing. Would this be their last dance? Or would there be other opportunities for her to waltz with Mor?

Before she could fathom out an answer, Wrae and Lochlen, and the other professional dancers, came over to them.

'Thank you all for coming along this evening,' said Lochlen. 'It added to the exciting atmosphere, and lots of folk got to skirl around the dance floor with a professional dancer.'

'And thank you, Lochlen, for making us welcome,' said Mor.

Everyone began to get ready to leave as the ceilidh came to a close.

Lochlen escorted Wrae and Ferelith to the door, and the night air poured in as they stepped outside. Lit by the glow of the lanterns hanging outside the premises, they said their goodnights.

'I'll drop off the kilt in the morning,' Mor called to Ferelith.

She nodded and waved, and then walked up to the shop with Wrae to where their car was parked. They'd kept to soft drinks during the evening, and Ferelith drove them home.

'What a night!' Wrae said, relaxing back in the passenger seat as Ferelith drove through the heart of the city, and then took the road that led to their cottage on the outskirts. 'Lochlen is going to put clips of the dancing and your piano playing on the eatery's website. I'm excited to see them, though I hope I won't cringe seeing myself Highland dancing.'

'You certainly won't,' Ferelith assured her.

They chatted about the ceilidh, and about the journalist's interview.

'Do you think he will turn up at the shop tomorrow morning to see the piano in the shop and the costumes?' said Wrae.

'I do. But he did say that he wanted to discuss with his editor about expanding the story into a full feature in the paper's weekly magazine supplement.'

'Did he?' Wrae sounded hopeful. 'That would be wonderful publicity for our shop.'

'It would. We'll make sure we're there early so we're ready for the interview. And Mor says he'll drop his kilt off so I can add sparkle to it.'

'Fine, every task that we can get done keeps us on schedule. And maybe Mor will have his picture taken in the shop for the feature. That would certainly gain people's interest.'

'What do you think we should wear?' Wrae said as they arrived at the cottage.

Ferelith parked the car and they stepped out into the fragrant air of the garden.

'You really suit your light yellow shift dress,' said Ferelith. She unlocked the front door and they stepped inside.

'I always feel dressy but comfortable in it, and it's one of our own designs, so I'll wear that. What about you?'

'I don't know if I should wear my pink wrap tea dress.' This was one of her designs. She laughed. 'I'd match the piano.'

They flicked the cosy lamps on in the cottage and headed through to their respective bedrooms, both digging out what they planned to wear.

Ferelith brought her pink dress through on a hanger to show Wrae. 'What do you think? Go for the pink? Tone in with the piano?' she added with a smile.

'Yes, it's such a pretty dress, and it's your own pattern,' said Wrae.

Twirling the dress around on the hanger, Ferelith nodded firmly. Decision made. She'd wear the pink one.

Wrae checked the shop's website for messages and realised they had someone coming along to talk to them in the morning.

'I forgot we had a client popping in tomorrow morning to discuss costumes for one of her new stage plays,' Wrae said to Ferelith. 'I agreed recently that we'd tackle making the costumes for the actors and the dancers in the play.'

'Is she the play's director?' said Ferelith, taking an interest in the forthcoming project that was probably going to overlap with creating the costumes for Mor. But that was one of the main reasons why Wrae was keen to have Ferelith join her in the shop, so that they could expand their business.

'No, she's the playwright, Huntine Grey.'

CHAPTER TEN

A bright, cobalt blue sky arched over the heart of Edinburgh, and the city looked magnificent in the summer sunshine. A heat haze softened the outlines of the architecture, and sunlight glinted off the front window of the theatre costume shop, creating a welcoming glow to the premises.

Ferelith and Wrae had arrived early at their shop to prepare for the busy day, wearing their dresses as planned. They'd stopped at the grocery shop on the way to buy fresh milk for making tea, and a tin of shortbread petticoat tails.

Empty biscuit tins and assorted toffee tins were used as pretty containers in the shop to hold everything from spools of thread to knick–knacks for sewing. The shortbread tin had a classic design and once it was empty it would join the other tins on the shelves. They were particularly handy for the haberdashery to store various items such as skeins of embroidery thread, tiny decorative pom poms and fancy trims. Along with the tins, there were old–fashioned sweetie jars filled with all sorts of buttons and beads. Many of these jars dated back to when their grandparents owned the shop, and offered a comforting sense of history to the modern aspects of the shop.

The shop was always tidy, but they'd made sure it was extra neat, and that the rails of costumes showed Mor's designs for the journalist to photograph. The blue ballgown sparkled under the lights, as did the pink and red versions of Torra's dresses that were embellished with sequins.

A mannequin wore the gold glitter illusion dress. Another mannequin had the unfinished version using the pink sparkle fabric. Both the illusion dresses were beside the haberdashery to hopefully be included in the shots of the piano.

Ferelith's desk was set with her artist illustration pens and fine white paper ready to sketch designs for Huntine Grey, and to show the journalist her methods of designing the patterns.

Wrae planned to sketch illustrations too for Huntine, and she had her large sketch pad on her desk ready to draw the designs that were needed for the new play.

The pink piano was set with a sheet of music, and the haberdashery was particularly well–stocked with rolls of ribbon and trims.

A delivery of new fabric, including a gorgeous range of silk and shimmering chiffon had been unpacked, and the bolts of fabric were added to the colourful array on the shelves.

Both their sewing machines were threaded and Wrae had already started machining the rolled hem of a chiffon dress, so if this was included in the photographs, it would show the shop in full working mode.

Spotlights highlighted all the areas of the shop, giving the journalist scope to include whatever suited the feature he was due to write.

'When is Huntine Grey scheduled to arrive this morning?' Ferelith said as she machined the seams of a dress, making short work of the task. This wasn't for Mor's show. It was for another client due to put on a drama in one of the theatres. Almost all the costumes for this client were complete, but currently the tasks were overlapping from finishing the previous customer's clothes to creating new designs for Mor, and now for Huntine.

'No specific time. When I spoke to her on the phone I told her to pop in this morning. I didn't expect us to be interviewed by the press, or have Mor dropping by,' Wrae explained.

'It's fine. We'll handle them all.'

Wrae finished trimming the fringing on the hemline of a dress and then hung it up on a rail. 'I told Huntine we'd sketch a range of ideas for her when she was here.' This was the usual practise when discussing what a client wanted for their costumes.

'What type of play is it? You mentioned it had dancing in it.'

'It's a dramatic stage play with romance and dancing. Huntine says she'll bring the show's brief with her so we can see the storyline. Her recent plays have been successful, and she's working again with her stage director, Cambeul. He recommended our shop to Huntine. I made a couple of costumes last year for one of his theatre shows. Cambeul is busy this week, so she's coming to chat to us on her own. Then we'll have another meeting with both of them.'

'As she wrote the play, we'll be able to find out what type of theme she needs for the show,' said Ferelith. 'What's she like? Easy to chat to?'

'Yes, she's very nice. She's about the same age as us, and has already found success as a playwright. But her star is still on the rise, so I think we'll all be able to work well together creating fresh designs and sparking ideas for the costumes.'

Ferelith skimmed Huntine's website. 'I notice she writes song lyrics too, and seems to be doing really well with those. And she writes novels.'

'Yes, she's known as a wordsmith. She writes all sorts of things. I heard her being interviewed on the Mullcairn radio show with Dair, the dancer. Huntine wrote the lyrics for his new songs. Dair sings and plays the songs as part of his new dance show that's on tour all over Scotland.'

'I've seen videos and clips of Dair's dancing. What a talent he is. As is Mor, but they're both quite different in their looks and styles. Dair's dance show looks great from the snippets I've seen advertised. It's put me in the mood to get tickets.'

'We'll do that,' said Wrae. 'Dair's dance show is on tour at the moment, but I'm sure there will be dates where we can go and watch him perform here in Edinburgh. And we'll certainly go to watch Mor's show.'

'Mor told me last night that he'd like us to attend the dress rehearsals at the theatre where he'll be performing,' said Ferelith.

'Clients often want us to do that, especially if there are changes needing made to the costumes. I enjoy having a preview of the shows.'

The shop's buzzer sounded, interrupting their conversation.

Ferelith checked the monitor. 'It's Mor.' She hurried to let him in.

'Morning,' he said, stepping inside. He had the kilt folded in a bag and handed it to Ferelith. 'Here's my kilt, ready to be sparkliefied. If there is such a word.'

'Sparkliefied sounds like a great word,' Ferelith said, happy to use it.

'We have a wordsmith due to arrive at the shop this morning,' Wrae told him. 'If she'd been here we could've asked her if it was a word or not. But let's make it one.'

'A wordsmith?' Mor sounded interested.

'Yes, she's a playwright,' said Wrae. 'We're going to make the costumes for her new stage play. Perhaps you've heard of her. Huntine Grey.'

He looked pleasantly surprised. 'I do know her, or know of her. I've seen one of her plays, though I haven't met her in person. In our industry, everyone knows everyone else, if not personally, then by reputation and their success. Huntine has been working with Dair, writing the lyrics for his songs. He performs them live on stage during his new dance show. I know Dair, he's a wonderful dancer and performer.'

'We have the journalist due to arrive this morning as well,' Ferelith reminded him, sounding excited.

'I brought one of the show's posters for you,' he said. 'It's in the bag.'

Peeking into the bag, Ferelith saw the poster rolled up and tucked down the side. She lifted it out and unrolled it. 'This is a fantastic picture of you. The movement, the colour, it's so dynamic.'

Wrae came over for a look. 'Oh, yes, what a great poster.'

'We'll pin it up in the shop.' Ferelith took it over to one of the walls where three other show posters were displayed. Their shop had designed the costumes for the shows.

'I'll pin the poster up for you,' Wrae offered, letting Ferelith get on with the kilt work.

Ferelith took the kilt out of the bag, laid it on a table, and was wondering where to add the sparkle. 'Do you want a shimmering glitter effect? Or lots of sequins scattered on the kilt?'

Mor frowned. 'I'm not sure. What would you advise?'

'Put the kilt on.' Ferelith handed it to him and gestured to the changing room. 'I'll cut a strip of sequins and pin them on so we can see the effect.'

Taking the kilt into the changing room, he pulled the curtain shut, took off his smart black trousers that he wore with a white shirt and dark waistcoat, and put the kilt on. The tartan was in shades of blue.

The shop's buzzer sounded again and this time it was Huntine Grey.

Wrae opened the door. 'Come in.'

Huntine stepped inside. Elegantly dressed, she wore a pale grey wrap dress, that matched her eyes, and her blonde hair fell in soft waves around her shoulders. She was a timeless beauty with lovely alabaster skin, and her slender figure had poise, adding to her confident manner.

She hadn't been in the shop before and gazed around admiring the costumes on the rails, and the piano.

'That's a beautiful pink piano,' said Huntine.

'It's a new addition to the shop,' Wrae explained.

Huntine smiled, and then took a folder from her bag. 'I brought the brief with me.'

Before they could chat about the play, Mor pulled the curtain back and stepped out of the changing room wearing the kilt, shirt and waistcoat and his socks. He padded over to be introduced to the playwright.

'Mor, this is Huntine Grey,' said Wrae. 'We're planning to design the costumes for Huntine's new stage play.'

'Pleased to meet you,' he said. 'I saw your last play here in Edinburgh. I thoroughly enjoyed it.'

'Thank you, Mor,' Huntine said, smiling at him as he shook hands with her. 'I saw you dance on stage at a performance late last year.'

'Ferelith and Wrae are making the costumes for my forthcoming dance show,' he said.

'These are some of the costumes.' Ferelith gestured to the dresses on the rails.

'Gorgeous,' said Huntine, going over for a closer look. 'I'd love some sparkle and glamour added to the play's costumes for the dance routines.'

'You're having dancing in your play?' Mor sounded intrigued.

'I am,' Huntine confirmed. 'I've written a romantic drama with dance as part of the storyline. I'm working with my stage director, Cambeul, and Dair is creating the choreography.'

'Dair is an outstanding dancer,' said Mor.

'He is,' Huntine agreed.

They spoke for a few minutes about their respective shows and the costume designs. It transpired that they both used the dance studio's facilities for their rehearsals.

'Cambeul booked the studio room,' Huntine told him. 'We used it before for my last play. The dance studio's facilities are excellent. We've probably just missed each other in the corridor as I know that the dance room is opposite us.'

'Probably,' Mor agreed. 'Pop in the next time you're at the studio.'

'I'll do that,' said Huntine, and extended the same invitation to him.

They were all chatting when the door buzzer sounded.

'It's the newspaper journalist,' Ferelith said to Huntine. 'He's doing a feature on us for the paper.' She then welcomed him in. He had his camera in a shoulder bag.

'Do you want me to come back later?' Huntine whispered to Wrae.

'No, please stay. He's mainly interested in seeing the new piano,' Wrae confided.

He looked around the shop with interest and made a beeline for the piano. 'What a wonderful piano!'

Turning round, he suddenly noticed Huntine. Smiling, he came over to chat. 'Huntine Grey! Our paper did a feature on you, Cambeul and Dair fairly recently for your last stage play. And your involvement in the lyric writing for Dair's songs.'

'That's right,' said Huntine. 'It was a great feature.'

'Are you involved in Mor's dance show?' he said.

'No, I'm here to have the costumes designed for my new play,' Huntine explained to the journalist.

'Maybe I can chat to you about this while you're here?' he said.

'Yes, I'd be happy to chat,' Huntine confirmed.

Smiling, he then told Ferelith and Wrae the news. 'I spoke to my editor about the interview, and he wants to put it in the paper's magazine supplement. He thinks it'll be an interesting feature. And it'll allow me to expand on the editorial and pics. The interview and extra pics will be featured on the paper's website too.'

Ferelith and Wrae exchanged a surreptitious excited glance.

'It'll include the interview and pics from last night's ceilidh,' he added to Mor.

'Wonderful,' Mor said to him.

'Does anyone want a cup of tea?' Wrae offered.

Everyone did, and Wrae went through to the kitchen to put the kettle on while the journalist took pictures of Ferelith sitting playing the piano. Mor was included in a couple of the shots, standing beside the piano wearing his kilt, making sure his socks were hidden from view.

Huntine kept out of the way and sat over at Ferelith's desk, browsing through a folder of her illustration designs, while the interview whirled around her.

Wrae carried a tray through with cups of tea and a plate of shortbread and put it down on a table for everyone to help themselves.

The journalist noticed Mor's show poster on the wall. 'Can I get a picture of you standing beside the poster?' he said to Mor.

'Certainly, but I'll change into my other clothes,' said Mor.

'No, keep the kilt on. I'll crop out the socks,' the journalist assured him.

The pictures showed Mor standing beside the poster, and a rail of costumes for his new show that included the blue ballgown. And they moved the mannequin wearing the gold glitter dress into view.

'Oh, this is gorgeous,' Huntine said, admiring the illusion neckline and sleeves.

'This is one of our illusion dress patterns,' Ferelith told Huntine. 'They're very popular for all sorts of stage performances as the sparkle effect looks great under the stage lighting and makes it appear as if the actor or dancer has been sprinkled with starlight and shimmer. The fabric itself is almost invisible, just an illusion of sparkle.'

'I wouldn't want to encroach on any of the designs you've made for Mor's show,' said Huntine. 'But if other shows include these illusion costumes, I'd certainly want these for the play.'

'They're not an exclusive design,' Wrae emphasised. 'We use our original pattern. Though every variation of the dress is designed for each specific client. No two dresses are the same.'

'Illusion dresses, did you say?' the journalist noted. 'That's interesting.'

'Yes,' said Ferelith. 'They're one of my favourite effects. But I love plenty of sparkle.'

'Ferelith is going to add sparkle to my kilt. That's why I'm here this morning padding around in my socks,' Mor told the journalist.

'Ah, I see.' He made a note of this too. 'So you'll be wearing a kilt with sparkle on it.'

Mor nodded. 'I'm wearing it for one of the show's routines that includes ceilidh–style choreography.'

'I'll probably sew sequins on to the kilt,' Ferelith cut–in. She showed the journalist the strip of sequins she'd cut ready to pin on.

The journalist noted down everything, his mind ticking over with ideas to add interest to the feature. He wandered over to Ferelith's desk. 'Are these your fashion illustrations?'

'They are,' Ferelith said, going over to show him a selection of the artwork. 'And these are Wrae's designs too.'

'I think our readers would be interested in seeing your dress design illustrations,' the journalist said, and then asked Ferelith to sit down at her desk, pick up a pen and hold it as if she was inking the artwork.

Wrae nodded her encouragement to Ferelith as the journalist took the pictures.

He checked the images and nodded. 'It's up to my editor and sub–editor to decide on what makes it into the supplement, but I think they'll want to include this topic. We ran a feature on fashion illustration before and it was very popular with our readers. Even if there isn't enough space to include the illustrations sufficiently in the paper's supplement, I'm sure we'll use them for the extended online feature.'

Ferelith felt a wave of excitement at the thought of this.

After taking numerous pictures of the shop, highlighting the piano, Mor's kilt being sparkled, and various costumes, the journalist spoke to Huntine.

'While you're here at the shop to discuss your play's costumes, could I take a few pics of you? I'm sure we'll be including an entertainments feature soon on your forthcoming play.'

Huntine smiled and shook her head. 'I wouldn't want to encroach on the others' feature.'

Ferelith, Wrae and Mor's expression showed they didn't object, and were keen to encourage her to have the pictures taken.

'It'll tie in nicely with the shop creating the costumes for your new play,' the journalist reminded her.

Huntine's initial demurral was soon changed to an acceptance.

'I wish I'd worn something more colourful and with a bit of pizzazz,' Huntine said as the journalist asked her to stand in front of the shelves filled with fabric. 'I want the play's costumes to have glamour and sparkle.'

Ferelith and Wrae exchanged a knowing look, agreeing that Huntine's grey dress, although classy, wasn't ideal to promote her play. They hurried through to the storeroom and came back with two full–length dresses that were prototypes of designs that hadn't yet been allocated for any show.

One of the dresses had the illusion effect and the neckline and sleeves sparkled with shimmering pink glitter. The other was a blue chiffon evening dress with shoestring straps that sparkled with sequins.

They held the dresses up to show Huntine.

The journalist looked hopeful that she'd wear one of them for the photos.

'A tough choice,' Mor commented. 'I think you'll suit both of them.'

Huntine nodded in agreement, but she knew which one she wanted to wear.

Emerging a few minutes later from the changing room wearing the sparkling pink illusion dress, Huntine smiled as the journalist took the pictures of her with the selection of beautiful fabrics in the background.

'Okay, one more pic,' the journalist announced, encouraging Ferelith, Wrae and Mor to stand with Huntine. 'Everyone in the shot. And smile!'

CHAPTER ELEVEN

'I'd better take this gorgeous dress off before I don't want to part with it,' Huntine said, looking at herself in the shop's mirror beside the changing room.

The journalist had left the shop to get on with writing the feature, leaving Huntine and Mor with Ferelith and Wrae.

'I don't suppose you could make one like this for me,' Huntine continued. 'I'm attending a ball in Edinburgh soon with my stage director, Cambeul. It's one of those events where I need an evening dress that's as glamorous as the occasion.'

Ferelith was pinning strips of turquoise blue sequins on to the front half of Mor's kilt to see if blue sequins gave adequate sparkle to the fabric. 'We do sometimes sell the prototype designs if they're not specifically for a show.'

'We list spare dresses for sale on our website,' Wrae added. 'This pink dress would've probably been listed, or we'd have reworked it, taken it apart, and recreated another dress from the fabric.'

Huntine's interest perked up. 'I'd buy it, if it was for sale.'

Ferelith and Wrae exchanged a nod, and a purchase was happily agreed.

Huntine was delighted that she now owned the dress. She stepped into the changing room and put her grey dress back on, chatting to them through the curtain.

'Are you attending the ball, Mor?' Huntine called through to him. 'Did you receive an invitation?'

'I did,' Mor confirmed. 'But I haven't decided whether to go or not, though I suppose it's an excellent opportunity to mix with likeminded people working in theatre, dance and entertainment.'

'It is. You should go,' Huntine encouraged him. 'Cambeul attends these events often, and I went to the last one with him. I met and mingled with lots of creatives, and one of them became involved in my last play. It's also an excuse to dress up to the nines and waltz around wearing a ballgown.' Huntine pulled the curtain aside and stepped out wearing her elegant attire again, and had the pink dress draped over her arms.

Mor looked at Ferelith. 'Have you and Wrae been invited?'

'We have, and we plan to attend,' said Ferelith. She'd finished pinning the sequins on the kilt and stood back to look at her handiwork.

'We've never been included on the guest list before,' Wrae explained. 'But our shop is gaining more attention in theatre circles, and we recently received our invitations.'

'Take a look in the mirror,' Ferelith said to Mor. 'Do the turquoise sequins sparkle enough for you? I think they tone in well with the shades of blue in the kilt.'

Mor smiled and nodded when he saw the effect the sequins had created. 'These are perfect.'

'You can take the kilt off now,' said Ferelith. 'I'll sew the sequins on by hand myself.'

'I appreciate the work you're putting into it,' Mor said, stepping into the changing room.

Huntine took the brief from her bag and showed it to Wrae. 'This is the play's storyline and main character breakdown.'

Wrae opened the large portfolio and started to read the story details. 'I like the dramatic opening. The costumes will have to match that level of theatrical drama for the beginning of Act One.'

Huntine smiled, pleased that Wrae sensed the atmosphere she hoped to create with her play. 'The costumes for my previous play were vintage quality. I'd like the new costumes to be dramatic but dazzling.'

Mor emerged from the changing room wearing his trousers, shirt and waistcoat again, and handed the kilt to Ferelith, being careful not to disturb the front of it where she'd pinned the strips of sequins on.

His hand brushed against hers as she took hold of the kilt, and for a moment there was that strong connection between them again.

Pretending she hadn't felt anything, Ferelith put the kilt aside. 'I'll work on it later and phone you when it's ready. You should come back for a fitting to see if it's suitable.'

'I'm sure it will be,' he said, and then quickly took her up on her offer. 'But I'll pop in to try it on again.'

Ferelith smiled at him and carefully put the kilt on one of the work tables.

As Huntine chatted to Wrae about her play's costumes, Mor sensed it was time to leave.

'Well, I'll let you all get on with your costume planning,' he said. 'I can see myself out.'

'Oh, you're leaving,' said Huntine, sounding as if she would've preferred him to stay.

He gestured to the brief. 'You've all clearly got lots to discuss. I don't want to be in the way.'

'Are you in a hurry?' Huntine said to him. 'I was hoping you could give me your opinion on the costumes, particularly for the dancing.'

Mor brightened. 'I'd be delighted to give my tuppence worth.'

The four of them sat around Ferelith's desk and began to discuss the brief. Huntine wasn't precious with the details of her play being revealed to Mor, considering him to be a likeminded person, and the press release with the storyline was due to be circulated widely by Cambeul.

'The play is going to be presented as a romantic drama. It's scheduled to do a few weeks run at one of the theatres in Edinburgh,' Huntine explained.

'You're not taking it on tour?' said Mor.

'No,' Huntine confirmed. 'It'll mainly show in the evenings with a few matinee performances. Cambeul and I want to be able to have sets that create an atmosphere that is at times deeply romantic, but glamorous. And we're adding dance routines to the storyline.'

'What type of routines?' said Mor. 'Ballroom? Modern stage?'

'Both, but with a strong ballroom element, giving us the opportunity for the cast to waltz around the stage in the ballroom scenes. The leading couple will also perform romantic dance routines within the story.'

'I'd love to sit and watch something like this right now,' Wrae commented. 'It sounds wonderful.'

Ferelith agreed. 'Drama, dancing and romance. I would really love to watch a show like that.'

'Those are the themes we're aiming for,' said Huntine. 'And beautiful costume designs.'

Mor gestured to the rails where his show's costumes were hanging up. 'I think you've come to the right shop.'

'I certainly have.' Huntine sounded pleased to have Ferelith and Wrae design the costumes. 'The fabrics themselves are gorgeous, and seeing your designs up close, I'm convinced you'll be able to make beautiful costumes for the play.'

Ferelith read another part of the storyline, moving on to Act Two. 'I see you have a lot of night scenes. These could lend themselves well to plenty of glitter and glamorous designs, especially for the evening dresses. It says here that you have ballroom scenes, but also impromptu moments where the performers are supposed to be dancing outside under the lamplights in the city. This provides plenty of scope for shorter dresses with lots of sparkle and hemlines like these ones.' She went over and lifted one of the dresses from a rail. 'The bodice is a leotard embellished with sequins and layers of chiffon for the skirt, varying the lengths to create movement.' Ferelith looked to Mor for his input.

'It's one of the dresses that Torra, my leading lady, will wear,' he said to Huntine. 'Apart from the dress looking great on stage, it's light and easy to wear for the dance routines that involve lifts.'

'The designs always begin with the character,' said Ferelith. 'And how the performer moves. Our grandparents taught us this. That's where the designs begin.' She picked up a black ink pen and began to sketch on one of the large sheets of paper on her desk. 'From your descriptions of the characters and the theme, I'm picturing dress designs like this.' She sketched a fashion figure, using long flowing lines that gave the impression of a woman wearing a dress with a fitted bodice that cascaded into a skirt with a hemline of varying lengths. It looked ethereal, timeless, perfect for Huntine's play.

Huntine looked surprised. 'This is what I had in mind. Lots of flowing fabric, and the dancers sweeping across the stage for some of the main scenes.'

'We would of course study the brief in detail,' Ferelith assured her. 'This is just what I picture from hearing you talk about your show.'

By now, Wrae had reached for her pad and drew another dress that looked like a vintage tea dress suitable for scenes that weren't for the dancing.

'I love this too,' Huntine enthused.

'It could work well for a classic modern stage routine,' Mor remarked.

Wrae got up and lifted a sample of a rose print cotton silk fabric from the shelves and brought it over. 'This fabric has plenty of movement in it while still having enough structure for the dress design. It's part of a new range we got in.'

'Yes, I'd like that fabric,' said Huntine. 'I know I have to discuss this with Cambeul, but our tastes are similar, and that's why we work so well together.'

'I'll put the bolt of the rose print aside for you,' said Wrae, stashing it on another shelf where they kept confirmed fabrics for the costumes.

'Do you have a colour theme?' Ferelith said to Huntine.

'We're thinking of a base of blue, with gold and rich jewel tones, like sapphire, ruby and emerald,' said Huntine. 'But we're open to suggestions.' She looked at Mor. 'What colour theme do you have for your dance show?'

'Initially my show director and I agreed on black, gold, silver and pastel tones. Then Ferelith introduced red into the mix, so now we're adding that too.'

'Mor's colour palette covers quite a range of tones, but we think it'll work well under the stage lighting,' Ferelith explained.

Mor told Huntine about trying on the shirt in the shop and how the red was introduced.

Huntine laughed. 'I know I'll have to consider that the costumes are suitable for all sorts of dance moves.'

'We use fabric with plenty of stretch in it,' Ferelith assured her. 'The men's shirts look like classic white cotton when worn with suits or on their own, but we use stretch fabric to allow the dancers plenty of movement.'

'This is important for the energetic dances and the lifts,' said Mor.

They continued to discuss the dancing and the play.

'I'm having to juggle creating more plays this year than I'd planned,' said Huntine. 'But this is what I've always wanted. I had plays written that are now going into production. It's a busy schedule. Happily so.'

'You must be very busy with your writing,' Ferelith remarked. 'How many plays have you written?'

'A fair few,' Huntine confided with a smile. 'I love writing. When I'm not writing for work, I have a tendency to write to relax. I had a stash of plays I'd written and tucked away.'

'I love sewing and dressmaking,' said Wrae. 'At home, Ferelith and I have fabric stashes and sew for relaxation.'

'Our wardrobes are filled with clothes we've made,' Ferelith added.

'I'm the same when it comes to my dancing,' said Mor. 'Even after a day of dance rehearsals, I'll go home and have dinner, then later I'll relax by dancing in the makeshift dance floor in my living room.'

They laughed, and continued to chat about their plans for the shows.

'I'll make another round of tea,' Ferelith said after a little while, and went through to the kitchen to make it.

Mor wandered through to join her.

Wrae was showing Huntine a selection of fabrics for the costumes.

'Are they dating?' Huntine whispered. 'There's a definite spark between Mor and Ferelith.'

'Nooo.' Wrae glanced to see that she wouldn't be overheard. 'There's no romance, not at the moment.'

'The way Mor looks at her...it's unmistakable how much he likes and admires her.'

'Neither of them is currently looking for romance. They're both so busy with their careers,' Wrae confided.

Huntine smiled thoughtfully. 'I often think that when you stop looking for romance, that's when you're most likely to find it.'

Wrae glanced again towards the kitchen, inclined to agree with Huntine.

Ferelith put the kettle on to boil, aware that Mor was standing leaning against the doorway. She concentrated on setting up the cups for the tea.

'I suppose I'll see you at the ball,' he said.

'You'll see me before that. I'll have your kilt ready in no time. Sewing strips of sequins on fabric is quicker than stitching each one on individually.'

'I meant, socially,' he clarified. 'Like the ceilidh dancing at Lochlen's eatery.'

'It was a fun night at the ceilidh. I thoroughly enjoyed it. I'm looking forward to the ball, but...' She sighed heavily. 'Wrae says that the level of dancing at the ball is pretty high. I'm competent when it comes to waltzing, but I think I'll check online for the proper ballroom hold for the waltz. And I certainly won't tackle a tango or a foxtrot. I'll sit those ones out.'

Mor stepped into the kitchen, filling it with his tall, broad–shouldered build that was emphasised by his expensive white shirt and waistcoat.

'I'd be happy to show you the proper hold,' he offered, trying to make his offer seem nonchalant when inside he longed to dance with her again. But his offer was genuine, and he'd no intention of overstepping when he made a further suggestion. 'Pop round to my house one evening when we're both free from work. I'll give you a short course in ballroom dancing. Perhaps even entice you to tackle a tango.'

Ferelith's heart raced at the idea of going to Mor's house and learning ballroom techniques. It was already racing standing so close to him. And yet...she wanted to take him up on his offer.

Come on, she urged herself, be a wee bit wild. If she went to Mor's house, it didn't mean that she'd take things further than dancing with him.

'Okay,' she heard herself say.

'Great.' He sounded surprised at her reply, as if expecting her to make an excuse. It was his turn to feel his heart racing. 'We'll organise a date.'

Ferelith blinked at him.

'A mutually suitable date for you to pop round for the lesson,' he clarified.

Ferelith smiled and nodded, hoping he attributed the blush forming across her cheeks to the warmth of the kitchen as the kettle clicked off the boil. She made four cups of tea and Mor carried them through on a tray.

Taking a moment to calm her senses, she breathed deeply and fanned her face hoping to cool the rosy glow on her cheeks. The last thing she needed was to give Wrae and Huntine fuel to assume she'd been up to no good with Mor in the kitchen.

Feigning a casual air, she went through to join the others for tea.

Huntine didn't notice Ferelith's inner turmoil. But Wrae knew her too well, and there was no hiding that something had been brewing between her sister and Mor in the kitchen. And not just the tea.

CHAPTER TWELVE

'I can pick you up for your ballroom lesson,' Mor offered to Ferelith as they chatted outside the shop when he was leaving. 'I'm rehearsing in the afternoon at the dance studio in a couple of days, and will finish around five.'

'Okay,' Ferelith agreed. 'I'll be ready.'

Ferelith waved him off, watching him walk away from the shop in the bright sunshine. Huntine was still inside talking to Wrae about fabrics for the costumes. Heading back in, she helped unroll a bolt of aquamarine silk that they were discussing for the dresses.

Wrae gave Ferelith a surreptitious glance, wondering what was going on with Mor.

'We have sapphire silk too,' Ferelith added, pulling down a sample to show Huntine.

'Seeing the aquamarine and sapphire side by side, I like them both.' Huntine frowned. 'It's hard to decide which one to pick.'

'The aquamarine is a lighter blue–green,' said Wrae. 'The sapphire is a deeper blue. We could incorporate both into the colour palette.'

'They'd tone in well,' Ferelith commented. She held up one of the sketches. 'This style of dress would suit the rich sapphire. And the full–length dresses would really shine if they were constructed in aquamarine.' She gestured to the range of chiffon on the shelves. 'We have plenty of chiffon to tone in with both colours.'

'I'll go with both of them,' Huntine agreed.

These were put aside with the other fabrics that were selected as the initial choices for the costumes.

They made Huntine a sample pack to take away with her. It consisted of a copy of the illustrations. Sequin samples. A colour palette, created with watercolour brush pens on thick paper, showed rectangles filled in with each of the colours and variations of the hues. Fabric swatches completed the pack, and ranged from pieces of solid colour silk and satin, to chiffon and velvet.

Huntine put the sample pack in her bag. 'I'll show this to Cambeul and we'll have another meeting soon.'

'Ideal,' Wrae agreed.

After Huntine left, taking her new dress with her, Wrae was eager to know what mischief Ferelith had been up to with Mor.

'No mischief,' said Ferelith, tidying up all the fabrics that were on the tables, rolling them carefully and putting them back where they belonged.

'You've been up to something.' Wrae tucked their sketches inside a new folder for Huntine's show where they'd build on all the designs. She put it in her desk drawer. 'Were you kissing in the kitchen?'

The shocked expression on Ferelith's face matched the intensity of her denial. 'No!'

Wrae believed her, but knew there was something else going on.

Ferelith feigned interest in fabrics while she explained. 'Mor has offered to give me a few lessons in ballroom dancing so that I'll be ready for the ball.'

'Ballroom lessons?' Wrae's surprise resonated through the shop. 'Will you be going up to learn at the dance studio?'

Ferelith could feel the blush rising in her cheeks. 'No, he's offered to teach me at his house. He says he has a makeshift dance floor in his living room.'

Wrae smiled. 'Oh, that's why you're blushing. You're going to his house.'

'Only to learn how to waltz properly. I'd like lessons from a professional dancer like Mor. What an opportunity.'

'Just be careful not to have your heart broken.'

'The shields are still up around my heart, as strong as they ever were,' Ferelith insisted.

'Huntine remarked about seeing a spark between you and Mor.'

Ferelith blushed. 'Did she?'

'Yes, and I told her that you're not looking for romance at the moment.'

'What did Huntine say?'

'She said that when you're not looking for romance, you're more likely to find it.'

Ferelith flopped down on the chair at her desk. 'I could wangle out of the lesson.'

Wrae could see her sister looked deflated. 'No, enjoy being taught by a professional like him. Just don't put your heart in jeopardy.'

'I won't,' Ferelith said firmly.

The next two days were a whirlwind of costume designing at the shop. Ferelith and Wrae made progress on finishing many of the costumes for Mor's show.

They also fitted in a meeting with Huntine and Cambeul at the shop. The costume colours, fabrics and theme were mutually decided, and the work began on these.

The journalist had sent Ferelith and Wrae a message saying the feature was due out in the newspaper's magazine supplement.

Wrae bought copies of the paper with the magazine when buying milk from the grocery shop. They sat in the shop and read the feature, agreeing that it was an excellent piece of publicity for their costume design business.

Ferelith sent a message to Mor. *The feature is out now in the newspaper's magazine!*

'I'll let Lochlen know he's in the feature.' Wrae sent him a message. *The ceilidh night at the eatery is in the magazine. Our feature is in it too.*

A few minutes later Ferelith received a reply from Mor. *Great, I'll pick up a copy. Are we still on for the dance lesson tonight?*

Yes, see you at five. And I've sparkled your kilt.

I'll try it on when I arrive.

'Lochlen has replied,' said Wrae, seeing his message.

I'm reading the magazine right now. It looks wonderful, and so does your shop. Pop in for lunch today to celebrate if the two of you are free.

We're up to our eyeballs today with the costume work, Wrae told him.

Dinner tonight? Lochlen offered.

Ferelith has a ballroom dance lesson. But I could pop along.

See you for dinner. Come down when you're ready.

The messages ended there on a happy note.

Ferelith tried to stifle a giggle.

'We do not have double dates, if that's what you're thinking,' said Wrae.

'I wasn't thinking anything of the kind,' Ferelith lied.

Wrae laughed. 'The more we try to sidestep romance, the more it seems to be circling us.'

'Maybe Huntine is right after all.' Ferelith smiled, and then they got on with their costume making for a few minutes before their mother phoned in a face–to–face call. She was a soigné version of her daughters, with green eyes and upswept burnished red hair, and sat at her desk in her office at the fashion house in Edinburgh where she worked with her husband designing mainstream fashion.

They took the call on Wrae's phone.

'We've just seen your press interview,' their mother began. 'Why is Ferelith playing a pink piano?'

'It's a long story, Mum,' said Wrae.

'Ah, here's your father with our coffee and croissants. You can tell us both while we have our morning break.'

Their father was a suave silver fox, wearing a classically tailored suit, with a polka dot pocket square artfully draped in his top pocket and a matching tie adding a dash of flair.

Between them, Wrae and Ferelith tried to explain the situation, but their father cut–in and summarised it for them.

'You've been ceilidh skirling with professional dancers like Mor, and playing concertos on your new pink piano in the shop while wearing a pink dress to match.'

Wrae and Ferelith glanced at each other. It sort of summed things up, and their father wasn't one for listening to elaborate clarification, so they didn't attempt to amend his slanted and condensed view of the situation.

'No wonder you're both in the news,' their father added. His monotone remark gave no hint of whether he approved or not.

'And why were you wearing that yellow shift dress, Wrae?' her mother said, sounding mildly disapproving. This wasn't the first time the subject had been brought up. 'I know you say it's comfortable, and it's your own pattern. But you have to dress for success. Dress for what you're supposed to be — a top–class theatre costume designer. That shift dress screams casual. It gives the wrong impression. If your own clothes are designed for sheer comfort, this reflects that the costumes you make aren't top quality.'

'We design the costumes to be top quality, comfortable and practical for the performers,' Wrae said defensively.

'I know that,' their mother said. 'But you need to dress well when meeting clients.'

'Especially as you're in the spotlight now,' their father added. 'You can expect to be inundated with enquiries about your costume designs.'

Ferelith and Wrae exchanged a curious look.

'A feature like this one in the press will spark a huge wave of interest in your shop,' their father said assuredly. 'I've sent you a couple of dresses that your mother and I designed for the new season's collection. They've been couriered to your shop, so keep a lookout for them being delivered.'

As if on cue, the buzzer sounded, causing Ferelith and Wrae to jump.

Ferelith leaned over and checked the monitor. 'It's a courier delivery,' she whispered to Wrae.

Wide–eyed about the timing, Wrae hurried to collect the delivery, and brought the large parcel inside and began to unpack it while continuing the phone call.

'Ah, I see it's arrived,' their father said. 'The robin red dress should fit you nicely, Wrae. And the cobalt blue will fit Ferelith. I cut it on the bias for a flattering fit. Bold solids are currently very fashionable. These two dresses will see you through the flurry of interest your press coverage is due to stir up.' He sounded so sure.

Wrae glanced at Ferelith, exchanging a look that said don't start a ruckus with their father.

'Remember, your mother and I design fashionable dresses for real people,' he added. 'You create costumes for characters. Vastly different worlds. You excel with your costume designs, but you need to present yourselves well.' He smiled at them. 'Your mother has added a few fashionable accessories for you.'

'We'll go now and try the dresses on,' said Wrae, bringing the conversation to a close.

'Wrae!' her mother called before they clicked the phone off. 'Are you dating the eatery owner, Lochlen? He seems very nice.'

'No, we're just friends,' Wrae told her.

Wrae and Ferelith paused, expecting them to ask Ferelith if she was dating Mor, but they didn't mention this at all.

And then the call ended with smiles all round.

Wrae let out a sigh and eyed the large parcel. 'Shall we?'

Ferelith nodded without a hint of enthusiasm.

Lifting the dresses, they stepped into the changing room, put them on, and looked at each other before seeing their own reflections in the full–length mirror. Both dresses were midi length with short sleeves.

Ferelith's first reaction seeing Wrae wearing the red dress was one of surprise. 'Mum and Dad have done it again, creating a dress that's stunning but understated. You really suit it.'

'I don't wear much red, but I feel quite bold in this.' Wrae admired the dress in the mirror. 'Their fashion designs are so chic.'

Ferelith viewed the cobalt dress in the mirror. 'Vibrant, but classy.'

'That dress is sensational on you,' said Wrae.

'It's something, isn't it.'

They laughed.

'Let's see what's in the accessories bag.' Ferelith peered in and saw two handbags. Modern, mini, top handle handbags. She lifted up the one that was silver with a hint of gold. Suitable for day or evening.

Wrae picked up the bronze and copper mini handbag and smiled. 'I love these perfect small versions of larger handbags.'

Ferelith opened the handbag and realised that there were several enticing items inside it, including makeup. 'Mum's added lipstick and blusher to this bag, and a coin for good luck and prosperity.'

'What colour of lipstick have you got?' Wrae's lipstick was soft rose pink with a touch of shimmer.

'I'd describe mine as amber gold. I never wear shades like this. I prefer your colour.' But she leaned into the mirror, put a slick of lipstick on, and blinked when she realised it was lovely and flattered her. She then swept a brush of blusher, that toned in with the lipstick, across her cheeks. 'Oh, yes, this is nice. My cheeks look sun–kissed.'

Ferelith then used the sparkling hair clasp to pin her hair up.

A similar style of clasp, but in metallic gold, was in Wrae's bag, and she pinned her hair up too.

They were smiling, admiring their makeovers, admitting they liked what they'd been sent, when Wrae's phone rang. It was their grandparents on a face–to–face call.

'We're up in Aberdeen,' their grandmother said, smiling out at them. She was a champagne blonde with silver glitter strands, pretty and spry, and wore a Paisley print summer dress she'd made herself.

Their grandfather smiled into the frame. 'Hello, girls!' He wore a tailored pinstripe shirt, open at the neck, and his silvery–blond hair swept up from his pleasant face in a stylish wave. 'We saw your interview in the magazine.'

'Imagine our surprise when we bought the paper this morning, and saw the pair of you in the magazine supplement. You both look fantastic.'

'Thank you, Gran,' said Wrae.

'We're so pleased for the two of you,' their grandfather said, leaning in to be seen. 'We love the new addition to the shop — a pink piano!'

Ferelith explained how they came to add the piano to the premises.

'The shop is looking great, all those new fabrics, and the costumes for Mor's dance show,' he remarked.

'And you both looked beautiful in the photos,' their grandmother enthused.

They all chatted about the interview.

Their grandmother smiled mischievously. 'Are you dating Mor?' she said to Ferelith.

'No, Gran, but he's teaching me ballroom dancing tonight,' Ferelith revealed.

'Oh! How exciting,' said her grandmother.

'We bought an extra copy of the magazine,' said Wrae. 'We've put it in the archive folder where you have all your news pieces for the shop.'

'Thank you, girls.' Their grandmother smiled at them. 'We'll speak soon.'

The grandparents waved at them, and then the call finished.

Feeling like they'd hardly had a moment to unwind from all the excitement, Wrae offered to make their morning tea.

'I could do with a cuppa,' said Ferelith, and then they both jolted when the shop's buzzer rang.

Wrae frowned. 'We're not expecting any clients.' They peered at the monitor. A pleasant–featured man in his late thirties, suited but casual, was standing outside looking eager to come in to talk to them.

Neither of them had ever seen him before.

As he cupped his hand and peered through the window, they saw a close–up of a press ID badge clipped to his jacket pocket.

They stared at each other and gasped. 'Dad was right,' said Wrae. 'The press are here!'

Relieved that they were well–dressed for a potential interview, they nodded to each other.

Ferelith took a calming breath, unclipped her hair from the clasp, letting it tumble to her shoulders, and smoothed her hands down her already perfect cobalt blue dress. 'I'll let him in.'

CHAPTER THIRTEEN

'I saw your feature in the magazine,' the photo–journalist said to Ferelith. 'I'm with one of the other main newspapers.' He named the publication. 'We'd love to do a piece on you. Would you be available to chat?'

'Yes, come in. Wrae and I are just working on some of the new costume designs.'

He followed Ferelith into the shop, and gazed around, nodding, especially when he saw the piano.

'I don't want to take the same angle as the magazine interview, but I would like a picture of the two of you with the pink piano.' He took his camera out of his shoulder bag.

Ferelith sat down at the piano, while Wrae stood at the side of it.

His camera clicked several times as he took the shots from different angles.

'We're doing a feature on popular theatre shows. I'm highlighting upcoming theatre performances for our entertainments news. We want to include various aspects, from the music to the costume designs.' He wandered over to the rails of clothes hanging up. 'Do you have any ballgowns that you could hold up? I'm featuring the upcoming ball. Are you attending?'

'We are,' said Ferelith.

'Do you have any ballgowns? Designs you've made for shows, or what you plan to wear to the ball.'

'We've got ballgowns in our storeroom,' Wrae explained. 'They're not for any specific show.'

'Could you bring them through?' he said.

They selected four ballgowns from the storeroom.

'The designs are variations on one of our patterns,' Wrae said to him. She held up a shimmering lilac ballgown and a white chiffon version that was shot through with silver thread.

He took pictures of Wrae holding the dresses.

'Will you wear any of these to the ball?' he said to them.

'We haven't decided what ballgowns to wear,' said Wrae. 'But I do like the lilac.'

Ferelith had selected one of their illusion ballgowns that sparkled with gold glitter, and a rose pink confection that had layers of chiffon in the full skirt. 'I love this gold ballgown.'

He photographed Ferelith with the two ballgowns, and nodded when he checked all the images on his camera. 'These are ideal for the feature.'

They hung the ballgowns on a rail, and continued the interview.

'Can I have a quote from you?' he said, putting his camera away, and setting his phone to record their replies. 'What do you start with when you're designing a costume for a new show?'

Ferelith was the first to reply. 'For a dance show, everything starts with the movement, how the dancer moves, and the choreography involved. We choose fabrics that enhance the movement, that flow well, such as chiffon and silk, and design the costumes so that they don't restrict the movement of the dancer.'

'If it's a play, we start with the character,' said Wrae. 'The costume is built around the character, taking into consideration how the fabric and design will look on stage for the audience.'

He clicked the recording off. 'Thank you, that's exactly what I need.' They walked with him to the door.

'I'll keep you posted about when this will be published, but it'll be soon,' he said with a smile.

They waved him off, and then went inside.

Ferelith smiled. 'I think that went well.'

Wrae agreed, but they both needed to relax after the unexpected interview.

'I'll put the kettle on for tea,' said Wrae.

'It's been a whirlwind of a morning.' Ferelith sat down at her sewing machine and got ready to machine the seams on the bodice of a ballgown.

Ferelith and Wrae worked on the costumes for the remainder of the day, stopping for a light lunch of tea and rolls filled with tomato salad and Scottish cheddar that they ate outside the shop, shaded from the bright sunlight by the canopy.

The sun now created a warm, mellow glow as the day gave way to the early evening.

Ferelith checked the time. 'Mor will be here soon to pick me up. You take the car. I'll get a taxi home after my dance lesson at his house.'

'He'll probably drive you home,' Wrae surmised.

A wave of excitement swept through Ferelith. 'Maybe, but you should take the car this evening.'

Wrae nodded, and left the shop just before five.

The eatery was fairly quiet when Wrae walked in, but there was no mistaking the warm welcome she received from Lochlen. He bounded over to greet her.

'I hope I'm not too early,' she said.

'Not at all. I thought that as you're here by yourself, you might like to have dinner with me through in the private area of the kitchen. We can chat about the magazine feature without being disturbed.'

Wrae was happy to take Lochlen up on his offer. She'd thought she would be sitting in the restaurant at a table on her own, which was fine, but his suggestion was preferable.

'Come away through,' Lochlen said, leading the way.

He wore his chef whites, minus the hat, and she found herself looking forward to chatting to him about the feature over dinner.

The kitchen was larger than she'd imagined, and stretched back a fair way to where Lochlen had his own niche that was part office, but more dining area for having his meals in comfort and style.

Anticipating that Wrae would want to join him there, the table was set with a white linen cover, classic white plates and silverware.

'Can I offer you an aperitif?' Lochlen said as she sat down.

'I'm driving home, so...'

'I'll make us a refreshing fruit juice and sparkling mineral water.' He handed her a menu to peruse while he made their soft drinks and served them up in tall, iced glasses garnished with slices of fresh orange and lime. Sitting down opposite her, he proposed a toast. 'To the success of our wee businesses.'

Wrae lifted her glass and tipped it against his. 'Cheers!'

'You look lovely by the way in your red dress.'

She told him how she'd acquired it, and about the unexpected interview.

'When will the interview be published in the paper?'

'Soon,' she said. 'I'll let you know.'

After catching up on the events of their day, they selected items from the menu.

'Everything looks tempting,' she said. 'But I think I'll have the roast vegetables in lattice pastry with the bramble sauce.'

'It's a new addition to the menu.' He insisted on serving it up himself, but he was so fast and efficient, Wrae hardly had time to read the selection of puddings.

'Here you go.' He served up their main course and then sat down. 'So, what did you think of the magazine feature?'

'I'm still taking it all in. I read it this morning, but I haven't had a chance to sit back and relax to read it again. The photos were wonderful, especially the ones showing the ceilidh dancing.'

'There's a picture of you and me giving it laldy on the dance floor.'

Wrae laughed. 'Your kilt was caught in mid–swing as you burled me around.'

'One for the archives.'

His smile lit up his kind eyes, and Wrae found herself liking Lochlen more every time they were together.

Ferelith had brought a change of clothes with her, and wore a mid–length, floral print wrap dress and comfy shoes that she could dance in. She'd refreshed her makeup, and her hair hung in soft waves to her shoulders, but she'd tucked the new hair clasp in her bag in case she needed to pin her hair up for the dance lesson.

While waiting for Mor to arrive, she took one of the music sheets out of the piano stool where it was stored, propped it up on the piano stand, and started to play an étude, hearing the wonderful tone of the piano resonate in the silence of the shop. The étude was short, but had a high level of technical difficulty. It was an ideal exercise piece to practise her skill and technique.

She was still playing when Mor buzzed his arrival at the door.

Smoothing the skirt of her dress down, she hurried excitedly to let him in.

'I heard you playing the piano. It sounded like a classical piece. Beautifully played.'

'I was practising my technique, playing a tricky étude,' she said.

'Could you play it again? It sounded lovely.'

Ferelith sat down at the piano and began to play.

Mor stood nearby, listening, enjoying her playing the short piece that filled the shop with its intensity of feeling. It was a mix of heartfelt happiness and musical melancholy that resonated with his current mood.

'There's so much emotion in your playing,' he said when she finished. 'That was a lovely piece of music.'

'It was in the piano stool. Whoever owned the piano previously played a wonderful selection of songs. I'm working my way through them in spare moments.'

Mor smiled warmly at her, causing her heart to react, seeing him standing there in the shop. He wore black trousers and an open–neck white shirt. Both garments were made for dancing, and the stretch in the fabric emphasised his fit physique. He'd brought the change of clothes with him to the dance studio to wear after finishing the rehearsals.

She told him about the photo–journalist turning up to interview them for another feature.

'You've certainly had a busy day, but I'll look forward to reading the interview.'

'I've finished adding the sparkle to your kilt. It's hanging up in the changing room for you.'

He disappeared behind the curtain to try it on, and stepped out looking pleased with the sparkling effect she'd created on the kilt. 'It looks even better than I'd anticipated.'

'Once the sequins were sewn on, rather than pinned, they merged well with the fabric of the kilt.'

Mor danced a couple of moves and watched himself in the mirror. 'I've got my sparkle swagger on.'

Ferelith smiled. 'Another job I can tick off your costume list.'

He matched her smile, and then stepped into the changing room.

'Leave the kilt on the hanger in there,' she called through to him.' I'll add it to the costume rails in the morning.'

'Are we ready to go?' he said, stepping out wearing his trousers again with his open–neck white shirt.

'Yes.' Ferelith picked up her bag, and flicked the lights off in the shop, apart from the twinkle lights that illuminated the costumes in the window display.

They stepped outside into the early evening warmth, and walked to where he'd parked his car nearby.

The evening had a sense of summer energy to it, and it felt like a date night with Mor. She knew it was nothing of the kind. But she couldn't shake off the excitement bubbling inside her. And she didn't want to. Tonight, she planned to enjoy her dance lesson with Mor.

He drove them away from the shop, through the heart of Edinburgh, to his house on the leafy outskirts.

'You've got a nice house,' she remarked as he drove up and parked at the side of it. The property was surrounded by a lush, green garden. Trees provided a modicum of privacy.

'It's handy for my work in the city,' he said, 'but I love the garden, though I have little time to potter around in it as I'd like.'

They got out of the car and he unlocked the front door. Flicking the hall light on, he illuminated a stylish house that wasn't too massive, and retained a cosy homeliness. Built on two levels, the house had three bedrooms upstairs, two with en suite bathrooms, and a spacious lounge where he practised his choreography.

On one wall of the living room, lit by the glow of lamps, hung a framed photograph of where he was from up north in the Highlands — Beinn Mhór.

Ferelith walked up to it, noting the name of the location that was printed along the top. 'Is this where you were from originally, in the Scottish Highlands?'

'It is, though I rarely get a chance to visit these days. It's a beautiful part of Scotland with magnificent views of the countryside from the peak itself. It's part of my past that I love, but I was brought up in Edinburgh. The best of both worlds.'

'Edinburgh is such a beautiful city.'

With beautiful people like Ferelith, he thought to himself. Seeing her standing there in his living room sent his senses awry, giving him a glimpse of what it would be like to have her in his world.

On the opposite wall hung the three fashion illustrations he'd had framed, along with his show's new poster.

Ferelith blinked, seeing the artwork in the light cream frames. The black ink, white paper, and cream frames created a stylish set. She knew he intended doing this, but actually seeing them hanging on his living room wall took her aback.

'I love them,' he stated firmly. 'Thank you for giving them to me.'

'I'm glad you like them. I've never seen my illustrations framed so well.'

He smiled, clearly pleased that she was pleased.

'I particularly love that they will last,' he said. 'You and Wrae's fashion illustrations are so different to my dancing. Even your costumes may become vintage pieces, or at least be worn again sometimes. In contrast, dancing is intangible, fleeting, moments performed on stage that are gone, like a bubble on the breeze.'

'I hadn't ever thought of it like that,' she admitted.

'But it's true. There are evenings when I'm dancing on stage, and the atmosphere is electric, the audience is caught up in the performance, the music, everything is in sync. Then the feeling is gone when the music stops and the lights are turned up, the curtain falls, and everyone from the performers to the audience goes home.'

Mor spoke so passionately about his dance that she didn't interrupt.

He rubbed together the fingers of one hand, as if trying to touch the magic that had been created on stage, to hold on to that feeling. 'There are some extra special nights when the dancing sparks so beautifully. Later, I can feel it in my heart, but it's not like your artwork or your costumes — dance is but a dream.'

She nodded, understanding what he meant.

'An average dance show lasts about two hours,' he said. 'A hundred and twenty minutes of starlight sprinkled over the stage, the audience, but gone when the lights go up.'

'Have you considered hiring a videographer to film one of your shows so that you can rewatch it, relive the magic? Huntine Grey told me that she's having her new play and the dancing filmed, and then making the video available for sale and download on the play's website after it's finished its run in the theatre.'

Ferelith's suggestion sparked his interest. 'No, but it's probably something I should consider. I'll look into it for the new show.'

She finally turned away from admiring the pictures, and smiled at him. 'What are you going to teach me tonight?'

'A classic waltz, danced with finesse and lightness of movement. I'm assuming you'll be wearing one of your wonderful glittering ballgowns to the event and sweeping round the floor.'

'I will,' she confirmed, gazing up at him, again aware that she barely came up to his broad shoulders. 'Maybe I should've worn higher heels,' she joked.

'No, we're the perfect height for each other for a romantic waltz.'

'Romantic?'

'Traditional,' he corrected himself. 'Though there is something about dancing a ballroom waltz that feels like the essence of romance to me.'

She agreed, and stood facing him. 'Where do I start?'

'Place your left hand lightly on the top of my right arm at the shoulder area,' he instructed. 'Clasp your right hand with my left hand.'

The feel of his elegant fingers holding her hand sent her heart racing wildly, and she told herself to calm down.

'You have great posture,' he said. 'And you seem confident and calm.'

She smiled to herself. Oh, if only he knew.

CHAPTER FOURTEEN

'I can recommend the summer pudding,' Lochlen said to Wrae as they decided what to have after their main course. 'I made it myself using berry fruits including strawberries, tayberries and raspberries.'

'It's sounds delicious. I'll have that.' Wrae put the menu aside.

They continued their chat over dinner, enjoying the pudding served with cream.

The staff were working in the kitchen, preparing the dinners, but the atmosphere was cheerful even though everyone was busy.

'I wonder how Ferelith is getting on with her ballroom dance lesson with Mor,' said Wrae.

'Wrae danced well when she did a ceilidh waltz with him. I'm sure she'll do fine at her lesson.'

'Yes, you're right. Ferelith will manage to pick up the steps and the techniques Mor will teach her. She wants to take the opportunity to learn the proper ballroom hold and the traditional methods of a waltz.'

'And remember, I'm holding another ceilidh night here soon. The week has gone in so fast, and people are already asking if it's on again. I hope you'll be coming along to join in.'

'Yes, I enjoyed myself. I'm up for another fun night.'

'Save a few ceilidh dances for me.'

'I will,' Wrae promised Lochlen.

'Keep your shoulders back, be aware of your posture, chin up, hold your core strong,' Mor instructed Ferelith.

She reacted to the authoritative tone of his voice, following his instructions, again aware of how tall he was.

His shirt was one of his dancer–style designs, and the fabric showed the contours of his lean–muscled arms and broad shoulders as he adjusted her basic hold. She fought to calm her heart, feeling the raw strength of his masculinity as he pressed himself closer to her.

The shields around her heart were being tested to their limit. An overload of this gorgeous man holding her so close sent her senses to a whole new level of excitement. Even if she hid this from him, the telltale blush rising across her cheeks surely gave the game away.

'Don't feel embarrassed. You're here to learn how to waltz. I'm not judging you,' he assured her.

She smiled, and looked up at him, into those blue eyes. His blond hair fell in sexy strands over his forehead. Her heart took another full–assault hit. Turning up the brightness of her smile, she decided to go along with his slight misconception of what was making her blush, and learn the proper dance hold.

'Keep your gaze to the left, over my right shoulder,' he said. 'A professional hold, rather than a romantic one where we'd gaze into each other's eyes.'

For a second, he gazed down at her lovingly to demonstrate the difference.

The shields took a rattling, but were still intact as he released his intensely romantic gaze and exchanged it for the professional look he was advising.

'We'll practise the basic box step,' she heard him say, while her senses were being rattled by the glimpse into what it would feel like if he was ever to look at her with real love.

'Concentrate,' he said, misinterpreting her hesitant expression.

Ferelith snapped out of her wayward thoughts, and forced herself to focus on the dance instruction.

'I know the box step. Though I always forget whether I'm supposed to step forward with my right first, or back with my left, or... Maybe you should instruct me and I'll get the hang of it once we're dancing.'

Mor talked her through the basic box steps. 'Step back with your right foot. I step forward with my left foot...'

Facing each other, they danced this several times without changing direction.

'Now repeat the box step, and do a reverse turn, that's turning to your left, counter clockwise.'

'I thought I could waltz reasonably well, social waltzing, but I've always wanted to learn from a professional dancer, like you.'

'Let me lead,' he said. 'You're getting ahead of us. Slow and steady.'

Ferelith calmed her pace and let Mor lead.

'I'll put some music on in a moment, after we repeat the box step, turning to the right. This is known as a natural turn.'

She followed his lead, keeping her frame upright.

'Relax your shoulders,' he said, causing her to drop them down.

'Step forward with the heels, step to the side with the toes,' he instructed her. 'Feel the rise and fall of the waltz.'

Then he stopped.

'I'll sort the music and we'll run through the steps again.'

She watched him go over and set up a few songs. The introduction to the first song started playing as he walked back to her and took her in hold.

Instinctively, she looked up at him.

'Look over my left shoulder,' he reminded her.

Ferelith adjusted her gaze, but her fingertips could still feel his strong muscles under the fabric of his shirt.

The music was a popular song from yesteryear and suited the waltz perfectly.

He felt her dance better when waltzing in time to the rhythm of the music.

The floor in the middle of the living room gave them enough space for him to sweep her around.

'Let me lead us,' he reminded her when she stepped too far ahead.

And as they waltzed to the music, she felt as if she was improving with every circuit of the small floor.

'It's quite a workout,' she said. 'No wonder you've got such a fit physique.' The comment was out before she could curtail it.

He smiled taking the compliment.

The first song finished, and the next one began, a faster song with a lively beat. She knew the song, another popular piece of music.

'Do what you've been doing, but up the pace, exaggerate the sweep as we circle the floor.'

Ferelith tried to keep her frame strong and remember the steps and turns.

Mor whirled her around the room, causing her to laugh as he lifted her off her feet at a particularly lively part of the song.

'I thought one foot at least always has to be touching the ground while I'm waltzing,' she said breathlessly as neither was doing this. 'I think we've been disqualified for the lift.

'Worth it,' he said. And then as the song came to the last few bars, he lifted her off her feet and spun around with her in his strong arms.

Her squeals were a mix of astonishment and laughter, enjoying his playfulness while learning a proper ballroom waltz.

Laughing and dancing, they waltzed around the room until the third song came to an end.

He released her and she took a deep breath. 'I can feel that my thighs have had a workout.'

'Not too tired to try a tango?' His sexy smile enticed her to be tempted, though she wasn't sure what tempted her the most, dancing the tango, or being wrapped in Mor's arms. A little of both, she decided. A lot of both she told herself.

Seeing Ferelith wasn't resisting learning the tango, Mor went over and put the appropriate music on.

Again, three songs that could play in order for her to try and pick up the techniques.

'I've checked previous news posts and articles about the ball event, and it's more prestigious than I'd first thought,' she said. 'Wrae can dance well, so I don't want to let the side down, especially as I think we'll be under scrutiny having been highlighted in the press.'

'I agree. If you hadn't been featured, those attending might not have known you made costumes for the theatre. But this is the entertainment business, and whenever anyone has the spotlight shone on them, people take notice.' He set the music to play and walked over to her. 'With this in mind, are you ready to learn to tango?'

'Probably not, but, I'll give it a go.'

Mor smiled at her, and then an intense look came over him as he stepped into tango mode. He clasped Ferelith, and this time she felt the difference in his hold from the waltz. A sense of drama and passion.

Her heart was about to be tested again, feeling his strong body against hers.

Ferelith went to focus over his shoulder as she had done when they were waltzing.

'Look at me,' he said, his voice a demanding whisper as the music began.

Eyes locked, they began to dance. He threw her straight into the deep end of learning the tango, using his strength to lead her in the direction he intended.

She'd seen the tango danced before, in films and show clips, so it wasn't totally unfamiliar. But the intensity of the movements threw her senses to the wind, and she found herself embraced in the sensuality of the dance as Mor took control of leading her across the floor in the dramatic tango walk.

'Keep your posture strong, and your knees slightly bent. That's it. Now cross step forward and back.'

They practised these moves several times, and then he added turns and pivots.

Mor led strongly, and the more she gave way to his powerful lead, the easier it was to follow the steps.

'Embrace the music,' Mor said, holding her in his capable arms.

The music was a classic song and she kept in time with the dramatic rhythm.

Combining the tango walks, the turns, and staccato movements, she let herself become entranced in the music and movements with Mor, loving the sensations running through her, both of achievement and the sheer passion of the dance.

She was breathless by the time they finished dancing to the first song, but Mor smiled and kept her in hold. 'Well done.'

His smile warmed her heart, while the look in his intense blue eyes as he gazed down at her sent her senses wild. But maybe this was what she needed, a night to let herself step into an uninhibited evening with a gorgeous man like Mor, and go a little bit wild.

As the introduction to the second song began, he steadied them. 'Ready to tango again?'

'Oh, yes.' She didn't even try to disguise the burning enthusiasm in her tone.

Playing off this, Mor raised the bar, and taught her even more dramatic tango moves.

When it came to learning ballroom dancing, she'd always thought of herself as more of a traditional waltz type. Tango was part of the ballroom dances, but it was a whole different experience, and one that seemed to suit her tonight. Or perhaps it was because she'd let her guard down for one evening with this wonderful man.

'I won't talk you through the tango now for this song,' he said. 'The tango is a dance that speaks through the intensity of the dance itself. Try it this way, express what you feel only through the steps, the movements, the sense of drama and passion.'

Ferelith nodded, and neither of them uttered a single word as they danced the tango from start to finish to the song, while their bodies spoke volumes.

Halfway through the tango, wrapped in a silent embrace with Ferelith, Mor felt his world tilt and open up to let himself be willing to take a chance on love. The feeling took him aback.

He knew he was attracted to Ferelith, though her feelings for him weren't clear. But even if he'd wanted to protect his heart from another wound when a romance had gone wrong, he couldn't lie to himself. If there was any chance of romance with Ferelith, he was prepared to take it. A summer fling wasn't his style, despite what others might think of him. And this tilted his world even more. Had he found, perchance, the woman to share his world? Or was the magic of the tango playing tricks on him?

The words of the song that was playing didn't help to still his feelings. A song he knew well, but hadn't taken in the meaning so strongly until now, when he listened as he danced with Ferelith...

I had other plans for summer
But she waltzed into my world with such intensity
I didn't want to be romance free
I tried side–stepping falling in love
Then I made her mine
A romance in the long, hot summertime...

CHAPTER FIFTEEN

'Let's waltz again,' Mor said to Ferelith after they'd danced the tango, completing her lesson for the night.

Ferelith took a long, deep breath, and nodded, still buzzing with the excitement from their tango. But she'd gone to his house to learn to dance, and he'd wasted no time in teaching her. The lesson was intense, and she felt she'd learned to improve her dancing.

'I'll play another song.' He went over and selected another tune. 'It's always a good idea to vary the music you practise to so you can adapt your dancing to whatever is playing. It extends your ability to adjust the steps, the techniques, and the rhythm of the dance.'

He walked back over and took her in hold as the introduction to the song began.

She recognised it, and realised it was a slow, romantic song.

Although the music was slow, her heart rate picked up pace, getting ready to waltz with him.

'The end of a ball or dance night often finishes with a slow waltz. Couples usually wrap their arms around each other and do small steps without any travel around the floor. And this is fine. It's romantic. But I'd like to show you an alternative slow waltz.'

'Do I use the same ballroom waltz hold?' she said.

'Yes, and I want you to feel yourself being swept around the floor, in smooth, fluid steps.'

Ferelith placed her left hand gently on his upper right arm and shoulder, and looked over his shoulder as she'd done before.

'Look at me this time. Make this last dance feel deeper, more romantic, create a connection, even if only until the end of the dance.'

The introduction resonated around them, and Ferelith looked up at him, meeting his gaze.

'Instead of dancing on the spot, let me sweep you around the floor, slowly, using the same technique as before.'

'But this time, you want me to look at you as we waltz around,' she clarified.

'That's right. I'll focus my gaze on you, while being aware of where we're dancing, circling the floor. At the forthcoming ball, it's probable that this is how the evening will finish. If you're dancing with me, which I hope you will, you'll be wearing your ballgown and waltz beautifully around the dance floor until the music finishes. Creating a professional performance for the last dance.'

They began to waltz, but the way he held her, strong but gentle, and looked at her, felt so romantic.

When the music stopped, they finished in close hold, and she was slightly breathless, not from the dancing itself, but the combination of the waltz and the effect Mor had on her.

'Thank you for the lesson,' she said, stepping back and smiling.

Mor ran a hand through his hair, clearing his wayward thoughts. How easy it would've been to have kissed her, but again, he didn't want to overstep the mark.

'You danced well.'

'I've learned a lot from you tonight.'

'If you want, we could fit one more lesson in before the ball,' he offered.

'I'd like to do that. I definitely feel that my waltzing has improved already. And I enjoyed tackling the tango.'

'I have a night off from rehearsals soon. Come round again, and I'll go over what we learned, and teach you to foxtrot.'

'Foxtrot!' She laughed.

'Yes, the slow foxtrot is a wonderful dance, and seeing how you picked up the steps and techniques tonight, at least give it a try,' he encouraged her.

'Okay.'

'Would you like a cup of tea and something to eat before you go? Neither of us has had dinner. I could rustle us up a supper.'

'I was going to call for a taxi and let you get on with the rest of your evening.'

'I'll drive you home.'

She went to object, but he wouldn't hear of her taking a taxi.

'Well, if you're sure. I would like a cup of tea, and supper, if you'll let me help you make it.'

'You make the tea. I'll make the supper.' He headed through to the kitchen as if he had a sudden spring in his step, happy that she was staying a little longer. He enjoyed her company and chatting to her.

Ferelith followed him through to the kitchen that had a more homely quality to it than she'd anticipated. 'I love your vintage dresser,' she said, admiring the porcelain teapot and dinner service displayed on the shelves, along with an old–fashioned tea caddy.

'It's been part of the house for years. I like the past, the quality of handmade furniture. The table and chairs are vintage too. The cooker and white goods are modern, so it's sort of a mix of styles.'

The kitchen was clean and tidy, but the vintage touches added to the homeliness of the warm beige decor. Splashes of robin's egg blue enhanced the vintage feel of it.

'I like it.' She unhooked two polka dot mugs from the rack and filled the kettle for tea.

Mor checked the fridge, which was well–stocked. 'What do you fancy? Sandwiches or a toastie?'

'A toastie.'

'Toasties for two coming up. Cheddar and tomato?'

'That would be tasty.'

Mor took two tomatoes and Scottish cheddar from the fridge, and four slices of bread from a fresh loaf, and began to deftly rustle up their supper using a toastie maker.

Seeing Ferelith busying herself in his kitchen making the tea, stirred something deep inside him, a longing for a real life like this.

Within several minutes, the golden brown toasties were ready, and the melted cheese and tomato filling smelled tasty.

Ferelith added milk to their mugs of tea, and Mor served up the toasties.

They sat at the kitchen table to eat their supper.

Ferelith chatted about wearing a ballgown.

'I assume it's one of your own designs,' said Mor.

'Yes, Wrae and I have dresses in the storeroom at the shop that we've made when designing other costumes. We plan to pick a dress from several that are suitable. I'll probably wear a gold silk and chiffon ballgown.'

'It sounds suitably glamorous for the event.'

'I think Wrae will wear a lovely, lilac sparkle ballgown.'

'I'm sure you'll both look beautiful. Is Lochlen attending the ball? Wrae seems to be getting on well with him.'

'I don't think he's been invited. Our tickets aren't plus one, so Wrae isn't able to invite him along with her. We're just going together, though we'll meet other guests, like yourself, at the ball.'

'Promise me the first and last dances?'

'I promise,' she said with a smile. 'Will you be performing at the ball? Dancing?'

'No, and I tend not to dance at parties and events. I don't want to look as if I'm putting on a performance. I just dance like everyone else, without any flash or flair.' He took a sip of his tea and smiled thoughtfully. 'Though I might make an exception when we take to the dance floor for our waltz, tango and foxtrot.'

'You're making me feel nervous. I think I can handle the waltz, and I've another lesson with you soon to practise and improve.'

'You waltz elegantly, and I'm sure you'll dance it beautifully with me.'

'I'll be relying on you to keep me right. My ballgown will hide any steps I mess up, and you'll sweep me around the floor, making it look easy.'

'What about the tango?' he said hopefully.

'The tango is tempting, but I'm not sure I've got the gist of the steps. And it's so dramatic.'

'We'll go over the tango steps at the next lesson,' he assured her. 'And if it's of use to you, I have video clips on my website of the tango, waltz and other dances.'

'I'll check those when I get home.'

They continued to eat their toasties and chat about the ball.

'I've looked out my tuxedo,' he said. 'But I seem to have waylaid my bow tie, so I intend to buy a new one.'

'We have bow ties at the shop, and at home, that you can have. Are you wearing a classic black tuxedo, white shirt and black tie?'

'Yes, but I'll buy the tie from you.'

'I'll put one aside for you. Our ties are made from silk satin, they're mainly self–tie, and the popular style is the classic butterfly design.'

'Ideal, thanks.'

When they finished their supper, Ferelith checked the time. Because they'd started the lesson early, it wasn't too late in the evening, but she decided to head home.

Mor picked up his car keys and they headed outside.

Ferelith shivered and hugged her arms around herself for warmth. The night air had a bite to it, and storm clouds swirled across the night sky, threatening rain.

He gazed up at the dark sky. 'A storm's brewing. I'll drive you home before the downpour.'

The drive was fairly short, from one area of the city's outskirts to another.

'That's our cottage over there.' Ferelith pointed to it.

Mor admired the quaint, but substantial, traditional cottage that was set in a lovely garden.

As they approached it, another car's headlights illuminated the road from a different direction.

'That looks like Wrae,' Ferelith observed, gazing out the window.

Mor arrived at the cottage moments before Wrae pulled up and parked beside them.

They all stepped out of the cars and stood for a moment in the slightly untamed garden.

'Did you enjoy dinner with Lochlen?' Ferelith said to Wrae.

'I did. He invited me to join him for dinner in the kitchen, and we spent most of the time looking at the feature in the magazine. The food was delicious too. How did your dance lesson go?'

'Ferelith was the perfect pupil,' said Mor.

'It looks like we're in for a rainy night,' Wrae commented, glancing at the dark clouds.

'Do you want to come in for a moment?' Ferelith said to Mor. 'I might even have a tie that would suit you.'

It still wasn't too late in the evening, and Mor decided to accept the invitation.

Ferelith unlocked the front door and they all went inside.

Wrae turned the hall light on and headed through to the kitchen. 'I'll make us a cup of tea.'

Ferelith showed Mor through to the living room and flicked on a couple of lamps that gave a warm, cosy glow.

Mor looked around at the living room that was a mix of comfort and crafting.

'That's part of our fabric stash,' Ferelith told him, seeing him looking at the neatly folded piles of fabric on a dresser and on shelves, along with folders filled with patterns. Sewing machines were set up on two tables, and there was a rail of costumes they'd made ranging from evening dresses to men's waistcoats.

'Organised messiness,' Wrae chimed–in. 'As you can see, we bring our work home with us. Or maybe it's more that we love what we do and don't think of it as work.' Then she went back to the kitchen.

'The latter,' Ferelith said firmly. She rummaged through a rail of accessories and found two ties. One was black silk satin, and the other was a black velvet design.

'I like the silk satin,' said Mor.

'Try it on,' Ferelith encouraged him.

He secured the top buttons on his white shirt and put the tie on, seemingly adept at tying a neat bow.

'There's a mirror in the hall,' Ferelith told him.

Wrae was rustling around in the kitchen making the tea, but she peeked into the hall to see him wearing the tie.

'Ferelith made that tie,' Wrae told him, giving her sister the credit.

'We regularly have to make several ties for a show,' said Ferelith, joining him in the hall. 'I was trying out new silk satin and other fabrics we've started to stock in the shop. I made the ties because we need them quite often.'

'I'll buy this one.' He took it off, rolled it carefully, and tucked it in his trouser pocket.

'Take it,' Ferelith told him. 'Consider it fair exchange for the professional dance lesson.'

Wrae brought the tea tray through and sat it on the table in the living room.

'Help yourself,' Wrae said to Mor.

He lifted up a mug of tea and a piece of shortbread. 'Ferelith tells me you're both wearing beautiful ballgowns to the ball event.'

'We are.' Wrae's expression brightened.

'I'm quite excited at the prospect of attending the ball,' Ferelith admitted. 'Mor is encouraging me to dance a tango with him as well as a traditional ballroom waltz.'

Wrae caught the look of friendship, fun and attraction sparking between the two of them, and smiled to herself.

As they were finishing their tea, thunder rumbled outside the window as the rainstorm gathered pace.

Mor drank down the last of his tea and stood up. 'I'd better get going before the rain starts battering down.'

Ferelith walked him to the door.

He patted his pocket. 'Thanks for the tie. See you soon for your next dance lesson.'

'I had fun.' She sounded cheerful, happy to learn more dance techniques from Mor.

Waving from his car window, he drove off into the night.

Ferelith went back inside, and Wrae topped up their tea, then they sat snug in the living room chatting and watching the rain hit off the windows.

'Did you enjoy your extended evening of dinner at the eatery?' There was a teasing note to Ferelith's voice. 'I thought you'd have been home long before me.'

Wrae fought to contain her telltale smile showing the extent of her enjoyment. 'We had a delicious dinner, and then we got chatting, mainly about the ceilidh dancing and the press publicity. Lochlen's very easy to talk to, and I feel as if he listens to me, and has time for me, even when he's busy. That's a rare quality to find.'

Ferelith smiled knowingly. 'You like Lochlen, don't you?'

The blush Wrae had been holding back would not be constrained any longer. 'I do like him. I like him a lot.'

'Lochlen clearly likes you too,' said Ferelith.

Wrae didn't deny it.

'But where does that leave Lochlen and you?' said Ferelith.

Wrae shrugged and took a sip of her tea. 'It's early days. I plan to take things slowly. Enjoy our shop being in the spotlight, have fun at the next ceilidh night at the eatery, and dance at the ball.'

Ferelith cupped her tea and snuggled up on the comfy armchair watching the sheeting rain run down the windows. 'I like that plan.'

'What about you and Mor?' Wrae prompted her.

'I felt myself in jeopardy a few times tonight dancing with him. Not from anything he did, but he's sooo handsome, a truly gorgeous man, and I like Mor. It's a potent combination, but I'm just not ready to let myself fall for him.'

Wrae nodded and continued to listen.

'Mor's world is starlight and sensationalism, and I want stability and steadfastness.' Ferelith shook away her mild despair. 'I know that's not particularly exciting or adventurous, but I've had plenty of doses of those and found them to be bittersweet, and endured far more bitterness than sweetness.'

'These past few years we've both been unlucky in love, especially you as you were willing to take more chances than me.'

'And here we are, tucked up cosy on a rainy night, having had the equivalent of date nights without any of the...' Ferelith's voice trailed off.

'True benefits,' Wrae finished for her with a wry smile.

'Not even a stolen kiss.'

'I don't think Mor would've objected if you'd given him a quick kiss,' Wrae teased her.

'I was thinking of things being the other way around.'

They giggled and drank their tea.

Ferelith sighed wearily. 'You're right about me being especially unlucky in love.' She looked out at the rainy night. 'I'm just not ready to play another game of romantic roulette.'

'You'll dance with Mor at the ball,' Wrae bolstered her.

'I will. He wanted me to promise him the first and last dances at the ball. I agreed, and I'm sure we'll dance a lot.'

'And at the eatery's ceilidh?'

Ferelith hesitated. 'It'll depend if he's free to go to the ceilidh, or tied up with his dance show rehearsals.'

'Mor made it work the first time, turning up a wee bit later on to join in the ceilidh,' Wrae reasoned.

'He did,' Ferelith agreed. 'But his peripatetic career makes it hard for him to be reliably available for social dancing, or dating.'

Wrae frowned. 'Surely no more than Lochlen's career.'

Ferelith tilted her head, trying to make sense of the comparison. 'Lochlen has a stable career in his eatery. He's not gadding about performing at shows.'

Wrae didn't entirely agree. 'Lochlen is tied to his eatery. He starts early in the morning, dealing with the food and drinks deliveries, bakes the fresh cakes and scones and preps the lunches. Then he's busy with the afternoon teas, and afterwards starts cooking the dinners. It's a full schedule. And yes, he's reliably to be found in his eatery, but he gets little time off for bad behaviour.' Wrae smiled. 'Or so he told me this evening.'

Ferelith nodded thoughtfully. 'When you put it like that, I suppose you're right.'

'Unless I'm mistaken, Mor said he's happy to perform seasonally at theatres in Edinburgh. These are only for a few weeks at a time. The remainder of the time, Mor is free most days, and evenings, to indulge in some bad behaviour too.'

Ferelith brightened. 'Mor is really only busy in the evenings, or occasionally for afternoon dance rehearsals. He told me he has no plans to go on tour, and loves being based in Edinburgh.'

'There are lots of wonderful theatres and venues in the city,' said Wrae.

Ferelith nodded and smiled. 'So Mor is quite settled for someone with such a starry career.'

With this bolstering realisation, Ferelith got ready for bed, as did Wrae.

'I'm still not entirely throwing romantic caution to the wind,' Ferelith said, turning off the lights before going through to her bedroom.

'No,' Wrae agreed. 'But maybe there's a chance for a wee bit of bad behaviour with your handsome dancer.'

Lying snuggled under the covers in bed, Ferelith fell asleep, listening to the rain patter off the window, with hopeful thoughts in her heart for romance with Mor.

CHAPTER SIXTEEN

'London!' Mor exclaimed when his show director phoned the next day to tell him the news. A theatre in London wanted them to come down for a meeting to discuss including Mor's show as part of their forthcoming performances.

'You know that I don't want to move to London,' said Mor. 'I'm happy in Edinburgh, and ticket sales for the show here are excellent. You said so yourself.'

'Yes, but you'd only be away for a few months. And it wouldn't be until after your new show ends.'

'No, I'm not interested. I have a chance now to make a more settled life while performing in Edinburgh. Perhaps next year doing a short tour playing to cities and towns in Scotland. Look at Dair's new show that's touring all over Scotland. It's a huge success.'

His show director couldn't deny Dair's success, and suggested a compromise. 'Come to the meeting. We'll fly down this afternoon, stay a couple of days, talk to the theatre company, the producers, see their shows. Then we'll fly back.'

'I have dance rehearsals,' Mor reminded him.

'We'll only be gone for two days, three at the most. Torra and Creag can handle the rehearsals for two or three evenings, depending on what you've got scheduled.'

After much discussion, Mor agreed to fly down with his show director to London in the afternoon.

Mor sat in his living room, feeling his stomach churn having to upend all his plans for the week, including Ferelith's dance lesson the evening after the ceilidh, and he'd miss the ceilidh at the eatery too. He'd done his fair share of touring and dancing, living in hotels, constantly on the go. His new show was supposed to take his career to the next level where he had more control of his schedule. So far, it seemed to be working, but now it felt like everything had been cast to the wind.

Sighing wearily, he'd agreed to go, so he phoned Torra and Creag to tell them the news. And to see if they'd help cover for him at the dance studio. It would cause less disruption to the rehearsal schedule if they practised the routines as planned.

'I can handle the choreography for two or three nights,' Creag assured Mor.

'Thanks, phone me if you need my advice for anything,' said Mor.

Torra was equally helpful. 'We'll manage the rehearsals while you're away.'

'I appreciate your help,' Mor told her.

Having dealt with the practicalities of missing the rehearsals, he now had to tell Ferelith he couldn't teach her to dance as planned.

Smirry rain created a soft focus look to the day, making Edinburgh's architecture appear like a watercolour painting.

The overnight rainstorm had faded to a light drizzle by the morning, and by lunchtime had eased to a barely there rainy mist.

Ferelith and Wrae sat outside the shop, sheltered from the rain by the shop's canopy.

'I love rainy days like this,' Ferelith said, sipping a hot mug of tea and eating a roll filled with cheddar, salad and tomato pickle.

'I enjoy sitting outside whatever the weather.' Wrae ate her roll that had a similar filling except with bramble relish. 'It's relaxing, but gives me a boost of energy to work for the rest of the day. I sat outside during the winter when it was snowing. Warm coat, woollen hat, cosy boots, and I've got a wee heater that I set up too.'

'I'm up for snowy days here like that, though with the recent sunny days, the winter seems so far away.'

They were still chatting and eating their lunch when Mor phoned Ferelith to tell her the news.

'London? You're leaving Edinburgh?' The surprise sounded in her tone.

Wrae cast her a glance, and picked up the gist of the conversation while she drank her tea. She could see that Ferelith had been taken aback by Mor's sudden change of plans.

'Yes, I understand,' said Ferelith. 'Don't worry about the dance lesson. We'll do it another time. And there will be other ceilidh nights at the eatery.' She looked disappointed. 'Well, have a safe trip to London.'

The call was short and not particularly sweet.

Ferelith explained the details of the situation to Wrae.

'He's flying off this afternoon, leaving Torra and Creag to deal with the show's rehearsals,' Wrae summarised.

Ferelith nodded dolefully. 'I suppose he has to work with his show director on various projects.' Her appetite for the remainder of her lunch waned, but she sipped her tea. 'I think I'm just thrown off–kilter. Last night, his plans seemed firm, so assured.'

'Mor probably won't take them up on their offer.'

'If he's prepared to drop everything and fly to London, he must be considering it otherwise he surely wouldn't waste his time,' Ferelith reasoned.

'Maybe he has to back his show director. We don't know how their business works.'

'And maybe I don't know Mor as well as I thought I did,' Ferelith concluded.

'Eat your lunch,' Wrae encouraged her. 'We've a busy afternoon ahead of us.'

Ferelith gave herself a shake, and breathed in the fresh air of the rainy day. There was a comfort to sitting there, sheltered from the elements, even when outside influences could so easily come in to rattle her.

But some intrusions were welcome, like Lochlen, hurrying towards them, shielding himself from the drizzle under an umbrella. And shielding the copy of the newspaper he'd brought for them.

'Your new interview is in the paper,' Lochlen announced, eager to hand them a copy of it. 'Don't get up, I have to get back to the eatery, but I saw that you were included in today's paper, so I thought I'd drop a copy off for you to save you getting drookit.'

Ferelith beamed a smile at him and started to flick through the pages.

'Your interview is round about page nine,' he told her. 'It's a corker!'

'Thank you so much, Lochlen,' Wrae said to him as he started to hurry away.

'I hope I'll see the two of you at the ceilidh tomorrow night,' he called over his shoulder.

'We'll be there,' Wrae called back to him.

As Lochlen disappeared into the smirry rain, Ferelith gasped when she saw the feature. 'Oh, my goodness. Look at the wonderful photos of the costumes, especially the ballgowns.'

'And us!' Wrae added, thinking that their cobalt and red dresses worked so well. She sat nearer so they could read it together, bubbling with excitement as each part of the feature that the photo–journalist had written revealed another aspect of their costume design business.

'He's quoted us too,' Ferelith noted.

The quotes were highlighted near a photo of them with the piano.

In all the excitement, Ferelith forgot about the situation with Mor, and went to send him a message. Jarring back to the current predicament of him leaving, she hesitated. 'Should I tell Mor we're in today's paper?'

Wrae didn't have an immediate reply.

'I don't want to look as if I'm desperately trying to grab his attention,' Ferelith reasoned.

'It's tricky. Maybe wait a wee while and tell him another time. He's probably running around packing his bags and getting ready for his trip.'

Decision made, Ferelith finished her lunch, and then they went back into the shop to get on with their costume designs.

They both sat at their sewing machines, stitching costumes that were part of Mor and Huntine's show designs. Ferelith added a fairytale chiffon skirt on to the brocade bodice of a dress that wasn't part of any particular era.

Wrae created a light as air chiffon dress, using a rolled hem to keep the edges fluid. When she finished machining the hem, she put the dress on one of the mannequins and stepped back to check her handiwork matched the fashion illustration of the design that was pinned to her work board on the wall beside her desk.

The chiffon fabric Ferelith was working with was shaded from a vibrant rose to the palest petal pink. The pink brocade on the bodice had metallic threads in the fabric that added a sparkling effect.

Within an hour into the afternoon, messages started popping up on their shop's website from potential clients interested in hiring them to design costumes for shows and plays, having read the latest feature in the newspaper.

Wrae took charge of replying to the potential clients, organising meetings, asking them to send more information, all sorts of correspondence stemming from the publicity.

Stopping for a cup of afternoon tea and a biscuit, Ferelith tried not to think that Mor was probably getting on a plane from Edinburgh to London. A shiver crossed her heart, and she drank her tea for warmth, ate her biscuit, and then pushed on with her dressmaking.

Mor looked out the window of the plane as it took off from Edinburgh, and gazed down at the city he was leaving behind to fly to London. And he thought about Ferelith, wondering what she was up to, surmising she would be busy sewing in the costume design shop. Perhaps playing her pink piano.
'...and I've told them we're on our way.' His show director's voice jolted Mor out of his faraway thoughts. 'We'll have an initial meeting with the producers and others over dinner after we arrive and book into our hotel. Then we'll head to the theatre to see their latest show.'
'Is it a dance show?'
'No, it's a drama, with no dancing in it. But they've invited us to see it, so I think we should attend. Apparently, it's a popular show. But the lack of dance in their schedule is why they've contacted us, particularly you, to add dancing to their entertainments listings.'
Mor relaxed back in his seat and discussed the various possibilities, downsides and benefits regarding accepting the theatre's offer. It was basically to leave Edinburgh behind for around six months and perform almost nightly, and during matinee shows, dancing at the theatre in London.

In the late afternoon a delivery of thread arrived at the costume shop.

Wrae unpacked it, checking the items and adding the spools and skeins of embroidery thread to the haberdashery, and noticed that the parcel included Ferelith's order of watercolour brush pens. Ferelith used the pens to sweep colour on to the costume illustrations. The black illustration lines were drawn in waterproof ink, and often colour was added to the artwork. Long, sweeping lines of watercolour were swept across the paper, showing the intended colours for the designs.

'Your new watercolour brush pens have arrived too,' Wrae said to Ferelith, causing her to stop sewing and check the pens.

The colours she'd ordered, included bright pinks such as fuchsia, cerise and purple, and a variety of blues from sky to cornflower.

Ferelith put her sewing aside for a few minutes as she couldn't wait to try the new pens, and added washes of colour to the recent dress illustrations she'd drawn. The colours were vibrant, but faded with a beautiful watercolour transparency into the designs, creating a gradation of tones that added an impression of movement to the costume illustrations.

Wrae leaned close to see the artwork. 'Oh, I love the effect you've created. It's a pity Mor doesn't have the watercolours added to the illustrations we gave him. They sounded lovely though the way you described them.'

Ferelith instantly pictured Mor showing her the framed illustrations in his living room the previous evening. She doubted she'd see them again now that he was likely to be leaving Edinburgh for London. And with his show's opening night becoming closer by the day, it felt as if their worlds that had briefly entwined were about to unravel. What a fabulous but fickle business they were both involved in.

At the end of the day, Ferelith tidied up the shop while Wrae finished sewing sequins on to the bodice of a dress.

Sitting down at the piano, Ferelith played a mellow piece of music, something from her past.

Wrae listened to the soothing melody and continued sewing the sequins. She was nearly done, and it was easier to finish a task like this in one sitting rather than tidy everything away and then set it all back up again in the morning.

Ferelith enjoyed playing the upright piano. The tone of it resonated in the quiet shop, and added to the soulful feeling of the song.

'I'm glad we bought this piano,' Ferelith said wistfully.

'You play it so well.'

Ferelith played until Wrae finished sewing, and then they both headed home.

The rain had stopped, but the city streets glistened under the streetlights as Ferelith drove them to the cottage.

When they arrived home, they chatted about what they'd wear to the ceilidh the following night while making dinner.

Wrae popped a lasagne in the oven, set the timer and prepared a green salad with a lemon juice and sea salt dressing while it cooked.

They agreed they'd wear the tartan sashes they'd made and worn the last time, but with different dresses.

Ferelith picked a blue tea dress and hung it up on the outside of her wardrobe.

Wrae opted for a mid–length, burgundy dress that had quite a full skirt that she thought would be ideal for the ceilidh dancing.

The timer pinged on the oven, and they went through to eat their dinner in the kitchen while discussing the ceilidh, and the stash of clothes in their wardrobes.

'We really need to have a total clearance of the dresses we've made and stashed in our wardrobes,' said Ferelith.

Wrae nodded as she ate her dinner.

'Neither of us can resist new fabrics, and we've got patterns galore, so it's fairly easy for us to run up a dress,' Ferelith reasoned. 'But I have several dresses hanging in the wardrobe, or stuffed in it to be precise, because of the overspill, that I've never even worn.'

'We could advertise them for sale on our website,' Wrae suggested. 'A special sale of dresses we've made. Not costumes, like the ones we usually list, but dresses for daywear or parties.'

'Let's do that. We'll tackle the task over the next week, and list them on the website.'

Wrae agreed. 'With all the added interest in our business from the press coverage, the dresses could be snapped up.'

They ate their dinner and chatted about the ceilidh.

'I won't be taking part in any dance challenges at the ceilidh tomorrow night,' said Wrae.

'Mor and the other dancers won't be at the ceilidh, so there shouldn't be any dance–off from Torra or the others.'

'Lochlen told me that he's expecting it to be another busy night.'

'I think it's more fun when it's busy, especially for a ceilidh,' said Ferelith.

'I'm sorry that Mor won't be there,' Wrae admitted. 'I feel bad that I'll be enjoying myself with Lochlen.'

'No,' Ferelith cut–in. 'I'm happy for you. We promised that if either of us met the right man, fell in love, and there was a true chance of real romance, we would choose love and happiness above all else.' She lifted up her cup of tea.

Wrae lifted her cup up, and they tipped them together once again, in a toast to romance and being happy.

'Will we have dinner at the eatery tomorrow night?' said Wrae.

'Yes, and I'm sure there will be plenty of delicious items on the menu. Lochlen seems to always be adding something to tempt us with.'

'And there's the buffet,' said Wrae.

'Delicious food and lively dancing. It'll be another fun night.'

It was a fun night as they'd anticipated. Lochlen had welcomed Wrae and Ferelith to the eatery where they'd had dinner before he announced the start of the ceilidh. And he'd had a piece of news for them.

'I've been invited to the ball. I received a message earlier inviting me to attend the event. They read about me in the magazine, starting the ceilidh nights, and seeing dancers like Mor coming along to the dancing,' Lochlen told them.

'That's wonderful,' said Wrae.

Ferelith agreed.

'I'll have to look out my tux,' Lochlen said chirpily.

The ceilidh kicked off with a rousing reel, and everyone danced with everyone else, and cheered when the dance finished.

It soon continued with the next song, and the dance floor was busy with people joining in a jig.

Ferelith let herself be enveloped in the fun, and pushed aside thoughts of Mor. She'd had an extra busy day at the shop with Wrae, dealing with the customer enquires resulting from their recent publicity in the newspaper. And they'd listed a number of their dresses, from their wardrobe stash, for sale on the shop's website. They hadn't anticipated such a fast response to their listings, but as people were checking their website due to the publicity, the dresses were being snapped up. As well as their costume making, they'd had to pack the dress orders and take them to the post office before heading to the ceilidh.

They'd relaxed briefly during dinner at the eatery, but now they were in full dance mode, linking arms with the other revellers and whirling around the dance floor.

Escaping from the dancing for a few minutes, Ferelith and Wrae had a refreshing soft drink at the buffet.

'All this relaxing after a busy day of dressmaking at the shop is hard work,' Ferelith said lightly.

'And the night is young.' Wrae sipped a glass of iced mineral water and fruit juice, but was then pulled playfully into the energetic reel by Lochlen.

Ferelith was about to laugh, when Lochlen clasped her hand too. 'Come on, there's a whole night of jigging to join in.'

With one on each arm, Lochlen led them through the whirling and skirling, and Ferelith's cheeks ached from all the laughter and smiling and sheer fun.

In the midst of a particularly lively reel, where everyone was skip–stepping around, linking arms for a moment, and then changing partners again, Ferelith gasped when she found herself being lifted off her feet by a strong pair of arms.

'Mor!' Ferelith exclaimed. 'You're back!'

Before he could reply, the dance separated them, and this hectic sequence continued throughout the fast–moving reel.

Mor wore an expensive three–piece suit, shirt and tie, and was so handsome that her heart took a hit just looking at him. Tall, and such a capable dancer, he stood shoulders above many of the other men, and repeatedly lifted her up without any fuss.

Ferelith's world was spinning from the dancing, and the surprise of seeing Mor, the last man she expected to see at the ceilidh night.

The reel merged into the next dance, another reel but less fast–paced, and Ferelith called to him in stolen moments when they were partnered up.

'I thought you were in London.'

'I flew back early. I took a taxi straight from Edinburgh airport.'

Then they whirled around the dance floor in different directions, and by now Wrae was wide–eyed, looking at Ferelith for some sort of explanation.

Ferelith shrugged, and the dancing continued for another two lively songs before Lochlen announced a romantic waltz as a midway break in the ceilidh to allow everyone to catch their breath.

'Shall we?' Mor said to Ferelith, preferring to dance with her rather than sit this one out.

She accepted his hand, and they began to slow waltz, and he told her what happened during his trip to London.

'They wanted me to do a full–season show in London. I would've needed to move there, and I didn't want to do that. I've been working hard throughout my dancing career to eventually have my own show. I'm happy living my dream, and planning to do another show like this, here in Edinburgh. I'm choosing happiness above all else.'

Ferelith smiled at him, as she'd heard almost the same words from her sister.

'But I've agreed to do two weekend performances for them in London sometime in the New Year,' he added. 'Then my show director and I caught a flight back to Edinburgh. And here I am.'

'I'm glad you're back.'

The waltz started to come to a close.

'You're waltzing very well,' he said. 'Great posture and hold.'

'I had a lesson from a great dancer.'

Mor smiled at her. 'And another lesson is on offer tomorrow night, if you're up for it.'

Ferelith nodded. 'I am.'

Agreeing that he'd pick her up from the shop like before, they finished the waltz and then stayed on the floor to join in the next reel.

Later, when Mor was talking to Lochlen, Ferelith went over to the buffet and helped herself to a refreshing, cold drink.

Wrae hurried over to her. 'What happened? Why is Mor back so soon?'

Ferelith summarised the details.

'So Mor's not leaving Edinburgh,' Wrae wanted to confirm.

'No, he says he's choosing happiness here,' said Ferelith.

'I'm pleased for you,' Wrae told her.

'And he's giving me another dance lesson tomorrow night at his house,' Ferelith said, sounding delighted.

'What are you two gossiping and giggling about?' Lochlen joked, approaching them and bringing Mor with him.

'I was telling Wrae that Mor is giving me another dance lesson tomorrow night,' said Ferelith.

'Well, let's all get in more ceilidh dancing,' Lochlen encouraged them. 'There's a rousing reel coming up.'

As the music changed to a lively beat, they partnered up and joined in the dancing.

By now, Mor had taken off his jacket and tie, and kept up with the fast pace of the dance.

Clasping Ferelith around the waist, he lifted her up and whirled her around before placing her back down safely.

Ferelith's squeals and laughter mixed with the music and sounds of the other revellers having a fun night, including Wrae and Lochlen.

As the evening finally came to a close, Ferelith and Wrae offered to give Mor a lift home.

Ferelith drove the car, with Wrae in the passenger seat and Mor in the back.

'I was telling Wrae that you've framed our costume illustrations,' Ferelith said as she parked the car outside his front door.

'Would you like to come and take a wee peek at the pictures before you go?' Mor offered.

Eager to see the framed artwork, Wrae nodded to him.

The three of them went inside and Mor led them through to the living room and gestured to the framed illustrations on the wall.

'The frames really show the artwork well,' Wrae acknowledged.

'Can I offer you both a cup of tea before you go?' said Mor.

They took him up on his offer, and while he went through to the kitchen, they chatted about their evening, and Wrae whispered to Ferelith. 'Mor has a beautiful house. Stylish but comfortable. And so handy to have a makeshift dance floor.'

'My show director and I had a chance to discuss hiring a videographer to film my dance show,' Mor said as he carried the tea through on a tray and put it down on a table. 'Ferelith suggested this. He knows a videographer and has hired him to film the dance show so that it will be available to watch after the run of the show.'

They helped themselves to the tea.

'That's wonderful,' said Ferelith.

Wrae agreed, thinking it would be an excellent record of their costumes being worn during a performance.

'It'll be filmed at the dress rehearsal in the theatre,' said Mor. 'You'll be there at the rehearsal to help with any adjustments to the costumes, so I thought I'd let you know that we're making a video of it.'

'Not long now until the dress rehearsal,' Ferelith remarked.

'Shortly after the ball,' Mor estimated.

'We've almost finished your costumes,' said Wrae. 'We'll schedule any further fittings.'

'Then the costumes will be delivered to the theatre's wardrobe manager in plenty of time for the show's dress rehearsal,' Ferelith assured him.

Finishing their tea, Mor walked Ferelith and Wrae out to their car.

'I'll pick you up tomorrow around five for the dance lesson,' Mor reminded Ferelith.

'Yes, see you then.' Ferelith smiled and waved as she drove off home with Wrae.

They discussed their dresses for the ball.

'I love making ballgowns for the theatre costumes,' Wrae said wistfully. 'But I'm excited to be wearing one of my own designs to the ball.'

'We should try the ballgowns on at the shop tomorrow to check that they fit and don't need any alterations,' Ferelith suggested.

'Yes, and then hang them in the storeroom ready to wear.'

Nodding that they had a plan, Ferelith continued to drive them home.

CHAPTER SEVENTEEN

'The gold ballgown looks gorgeous on you.' Wrae admired the dress, while wearing the lilac ballgown. It was late in the afternoon, and they tried the dresses on as agreed to check that they fitted well.

The gold glitter in the fine chiffon fabric sparkled under the shop lights as Ferelith turned around and looked at herself in the mirror. 'I don't need to make any alterations.'

Wrae agreed, and after making a minor adjustment to the straps on the bodice of her lilac ballgown, her dress was hung up too in the storeroom ready for the ball.

Their day had been particularly busy, not only from the costume making, but from dealing with the messages from potential clients that were still popping up on their website. And selling the excess dresses from their wardrobes that they'd listed for sale.

'Everything will quieten down again once the publicity wanes,' Ferelith reasoned.

'And after we've been to the ball.'

'Then there's Mor's dress rehearsal at the theatre,' Ferelith added. 'I'm sure we'll go to his opening night too.'

'We will. And we've made a start on the costumes for Huntine's play.'

'And agreed to help with the costumes for a Christmas show in Edinburgh,' said Ferelith.

'I love working with festive fabrics,' Wrae enthused. 'Lots of sparkle, ice crystal designs.'

'Glistening snowflakes and tinsel fabric,' Ferelith added.

'Plus whatever jobs we accept from the incoming offers.'

'We'll meet new potential clients at the ball too.'

Then they burst out laughing.

'What were you saying about things quietening down?' said Wrae.

'Maybe in the New Year,' Ferelith joked.

'At Hogmanay?' Wrae exclaimed with a smile. 'It's always one of our busiest times.'

They laughed again and started to tidy up the shop ready to close for the day.

'We want to be busy for the business to thrive,' Ferelith concluded.

'Now you'll be here full–time,' said Wrae. 'Double the power. Double the trouble.'

'Speaking of trouble, Mor should be here soon.'

'What dance is he teaching you tonight?'

'I don't know,' Ferelith said, folding fabric up and stashing it neatly on the shelves. 'We'll probably practise the dances I learned the last time. Though he did mention the foxtrot.'

Wrae switched her sewing machine off and put the quilted cover on it. She'd made the cover herself from a vintage print fabric. Their sewing skills extended to so many things they could make that were useful for their business while being fun to sew. They made their own items for the shop, like seat cushions, and other handy things for the shop and the cottage like oven mitts, quilted tea cosies and aprons, all sewn from spare fabric. Everything was made for fun or functionality.

Picking up her bag, Wrae got ready to leave, taking the car like last time.

'Enjoy your foxtrotting and waltzing with Mor,' said Wrae.

'Are you popping into the eatery tonight?'

'No, I'm heading home, and if it's one of those warm summer evenings, I might potter around in the garden after my dinner. Or just relax in the garden.'

'While sewing something,' Ferelith teased her.

Wrae tapped her bag that was filled with fabric remnants. 'I kept the velvet and satin off–cuts from the costumes. I thought I'd make myself a wee evening bag to go with my dress for the ball.'

'That's a nice idea. I might make one too.' Ferelith glanced at the deep gold velvet and satin on the shelves.

Wrae opened her bag to show that she had fabric to make one for Ferelith too.

'Thank you, Wrae.'

After Wrae left, Ferelith refreshed her makeup and put on the wrap dress she'd brought with her for her dance lesson. She'd just finished getting ready when the buzzer sounded.

Ferelith opened the door and let Mor in. 'I'm ready, but I wanted to show you this. While you were away, the new feature was published in the newspaper.'

Mor was keen to read it.

She admired him while he read the editorial, thinking how handsome he looked. His blond hair was swept back and he looked like he'd not long stepped from the shower. He wore a pale blue shirt and dark trousers, and her heart fluttered with excitement.

'This is a great feature,' Mor concluded after reading it and studying the pictures.

Ferelith smiled and tucked the newspaper away for safe keeping in her desk drawer, planning to add it to the cuttings that were kept in the shop's archive folder. Then she picked up her bag, indicating she was ready to go.

Mor led the way outside, and after securing the shop, she got into his car and they drove to his house for another evening of dance tutorial.

He set everything up in the living room, and the lamps gave a welcoming glow.

'Do you want tea or something to drink before we start?' he offered.

'No, I'm fine.'

He towered over her as usual, and smiled cheerfully. 'I know I teased you about learning the slow foxtrot, but would you like to try it? Then we can practise the waltz and tango.'

'Yes, I'm up for that.'

'It's a wonderful dance, and it feels great when you glide smoothly across the dance floor, combining elegant feather steps, reverse turns, natural turns, and other steps. It's a wee bit tricky but well worth learning.'

Mor took her in hold to commence the lesson.

Feeling his strength so close, and those tight abs beneath the fabric of his shirt pressed against her, made her heartbeat soar. She inwardly told herself to calm down and concentrate on learning the dance.

'Don't look so tense,' he said, misreading her expression. 'This is just you and me practising for fun, or social dancing. It's not a competition, and we're certainly not competing against ourselves.'

The only thing she was competing against was the urge to let herself be swept off her feet by him, and not in the foxtrot or waltzing sense.

He smiled at her. 'Relax, and follow my lead...'

She managed to achieve half of his request, and followed his instruction well.

'You're tensing up,' he noted, releasing her from hold. 'Keep your posture strong, but let go of any tension.' He gently pressed his hands on the front and back of her waist, instructing her. 'Breathe in, but keep your shoulders down and your core strong.'

She felt a blush give her cheeks a rosy glow as her body betrayed her, revealing the effect he had on her. It was all the more potent this evening, and she put this increase down to the events of the past two days, thinking he was leaving for London. Everything had been topsy–turvy. Now he wanted her to relax while her heart soared just being there with him, knowing that London wasn't on his schedule.

'You don't need to wind yourself up, Ferelith. Would you rather we practised the waltz?' he offered caringly.

Whether it was the foxtrot, waltz, or hokey–cokey, it didn't matter because it was the effect of him, not the dancing, that was causing her to blush.

'No, I'm just unwinding from a hectic day,' she said. Not entirely true, or complete fabrication.

Taking her at face value, he nodded, and then took her in close hold again. 'The foxtrot is all about gliding across the floor.'

She forced a smile. 'Let's glide.'

This time, she concentrated on learning the dance, realising that Mor was right about it. The slow foxtrot felt wonderful as she picked up the steps, the rhythm, and glided across the floor.

'That's it, you've got the hang of it.' He sounded pleased, and then continued to teach her the remainder of the techniques.

They finished in close hold, so close that his lips were a breath away from hers. And the temptation and tension between them sparked, undisguised.

Mor stepped back and did that telltale gesture of running his hands through his thick blond hair whenever he was as rattled or roused as she was.

'I'll put some music on and we'll run through that again.'

She watched him stride over to the music system, and flick the music on. Clearly he'd set up a selection of songs ready for the dance lesson.

As the introduction played, he hurried over and took her in hold. The sky blue of his open neck shirt paled against the intense blue of his eyes.

The music helped her keep to the correct beat that changed depending on whether they were doing feather steps or sways.

There were moments when his strength took charge and she felt him override her wayward steps by almost lifting her off the floor.

She decided that when she was wearing a ballgown, her futtery footwork would be hidden under the layers of sparkling gold chiffon.

'That's better,' he encouraged her. 'You're getting the hang of the steps.'

They danced the slow foxtrot another couple of times, and then he changed the music to practise the waltz with her.

By the time they concluded with the tango, she'd contained her excitement when he was pressed against her, held her close, and gazed down at her with those gorgeous blue eyes.

'Well done,' he said. 'You're dancing with more control and assurance now.'

'All thanks to your professional instruction.' She gave him the credit.

'Would you care to have dinner?' he offered, looking eager for her to accept, and when she did, and followed him through to the kitchen, she realised he'd bought in plenty of fresh groceries and that a toastie snack wasn't on the menu.

'I wasn't sure what to buy,' he said, looking as if he'd cherry–picked it all with care.

'Everything looks tempting.' Including Mor, standing there in his kitchen smiling at her, all broad shoulders and smouldering handsomeness.

'Pasta?' he suggested, knowing this was something he could cook quite quickly and easily, especially as he had a jar of delicious tomato pasta sauce that was rich with tomatoes, onion, peppers, herbs and spices.

'Ideal.'

He boiled a pan of water to cook the pasta, and encouraged Ferelith to take a seat at the kitchen table and relax while he busied himself rustling up dinner.

She took little persuasion as they'd danced for an hour and a half without a break. Though she didn't notice the time when she was dancing with Mor. It went in so quickly. And the exhilaration outweighed the exhaustion. No wonder he was so fit.

'You're frowning,' he said, jolting from her thoughts.

'I was just thinking that I understand now why you're so fit with all the dancing you do.'

'It's the perfect career for me. I love dancing, music, feeling fit and strong, and my work gives me everything I need.' He looked thoughtful, and now it was his turn to frown. Everything except a woman to love and share his life with.

'You're frowning,' she said.

Mor shrugged off his deep thoughts with a smile. 'Just thinking about the ball,' he fibbed. 'I've a full day and night of rehearsals at the dance studio tomorrow. Then the following evening, it's the ball.'

'I've a hectic day of costume designing at the shop tomorrow. We probably won't see each other until the night of the ball when we're all done up in our finery.'

'Is Wrae going with Lochlen now that he's been invited.'

'No, we're arriving on our own and meeting others, like Lochlen, when we're there.'

'I'd be happy to drive you and Wrae to the ball,' he offered.

Ferelith was going to refuse his offer when he added a further comment.

'I thought it might be tricky driving while you're wearing a ballgown.'

Her expression showed she hadn't thought about this. 'Would you mind if I phoned Wrae?'

'Not at all, and ask her if Lochlen wants to go with us too.' Mor got on with the cooking while Ferelith phoned her sister.

'Mor has offered to drive us to the ball,' she began, adding the details of the predicament.

'Accept Mor's offer,' said Wrae. 'We'll sit in the back seat wearing our ballgowns and arrive in style. I'll phone Lochlen right now, and call you back,' Wrae said, and then clicked the call to a close.

The pasta was nearly ready as Ferelith made two mugs of tea and sat them down on the kitchen table.

Wrae phoned Ferelith sounding delighted. 'Lochlen's coming with us.'

'I'll tell Mor.'

Ferelith put her phone away. 'Lochlen is happy to go along.'

'Great.' And suddenly it felt like a double date night for the four of them, though Mor kept this thought to himself.

Over dinner, they discussed what she'd learned at her dance lesson, the ball, and how close it was to the full dress rehearsal for Mor's dance show.

'I have your tickets for the show's opening night,' he said, reaching for an envelope that was propped up on the kitchen dresser.

Ferelith noticed that there were a few tickets tucked into the envelope.

'There are tickets for your parents and grandparents,' he added. 'I don't know if they plan to come along.' He shrugged off his thoughtful gesture. 'Or you can give the tickets to someone else if you want.'

'I'm sure my grandparents will want to come to see the show, and my parents.' She was certain of the first and unsure of the second, but planned to offer her parents the tickets anyway.

'The tickets are all meet and greet ones, so they can join us backstage after the show to celebrate,' he said.

Ferelith pictured everyone's excitement at being invited backstage, and her own at the thought of sitting in the audience watching the dancers wearing the costumes their shop had designed.

They tucked into their pasta, and Mor was interested in her plans for the shop.

'We've had a lot of interest in our designs from those working in the theatre, and have accepted a few jobs already. Usually, the theatres plan their shows months in advance, and that's what we want, a secure schedule of clients booked up. It lets us plan when buying fabric in bulk, knowing the shows we'll need it for. Some clients only want one costume. This afternoon we agreed to make a dazzling ballgown for the leading lady in a stage play. I've sketched a design and emailed it to them for approval. If they like it, I'll start cutting the pattern pieces soon and begin the dressmaking.'

They continued discussing her costume design work, and his plans for his dance show, as they finished their dinner.

'Thank you again for the dance lesson,' Ferelith said, getting ready to leave.

'I'm looking forward to dancing with you at the ball.' Mor walked her outside to his car. 'Would you like me to pick you and Wrae up at your house?'

'No, at the shop. We have our ballgowns hanging up in the storeroom, and thought it would be easier to leave from there after work.'

'I'll be there in plenty of time,' he assured her. 'And I'll pick up Lochlen on the way.'

Smiling at him, they got into his car and he drove her home.

It was the day of the ball, late afternoon in the costume design shop. Ferelith wore her robin pincushion on her wrist as she pinned the pattern pieces of a dress to the glittering silk fabric on the cutting table. The design for the dazzling ballgown had been approved by the theatre. She'd cut the required amount of fabric and folded it in accordance with the pattern layout. It was too late in the day to start piecing the dress together, but she made a start on it by having all the pattern pieces cut.

As Ferelith and Wrae had almost finished the costumes for Mor, they were starting to overlap into new projects, including working on costumes for

Huntine Grey's show. And taking on smaller tasks, like a one–off ballgown, that had come through from the recent publicity.

After the paper pattern pieces were pinned carefully to the fabric, Ferelith used her dressmaking scissors to cut out each part of the dress. These pieces were placed carefully at the side of her sewing machine to be assembled the following day.

Efie was in the shop, dropping off items she'd added sequins to and picking up the next set of costumes to take home. Several people had contacted the shop, after seeing the press features, and wanted small jobs done, including minor alterations, and sequins and sparkle added to costumes for stage performances. Busy with their own main design work, Ferelith and Wrae had given these extra tasks to Efie and the outsource machinists they worked with.

'Mor gave me tickets for the opening night of his dance show.' Ferelith took the envelope from her desk and handed two tickets to Efie.

Efie was delighted with the tickets. 'I'm going to take my husband with me. He'll enjoy the show too, and although Mor gave me backstage passes, the meet and greet will be even more special. I'm so excited.'

'Our grandparents have told us they're going,' said Wrae.

'And our parents phoned to say they'll go too,' Ferelith added.

'It'll be nice to see them again,' Efie remarked, folding up two dresses and putting them in her bag to take away with her.

After Efie left, Ferelith and Wrae continued with the costume making, and then finally tidied up the shop, and started to get ready for the ball.

Wrae wore her hair up in a classy chignon, while Ferelith's hair hung in soft waves to her shoulders with the sides pinned up with diamante clasps.

When the buzzer sounded, they smiled excitedly at each other, and picked up the evening bags Wrae had made for them, pouch styles in velvet and satin to tone in with their ballgowns.

They opened the door and stepped outside into the warm evening's mellow glow.

Mor and Lochlen were both standing there smiling, well–dressed in their suits.

'You both look beautiful in your ballgowns,' said Mor.

Lochlen smiled and nodded, and stepped forward to escort Wrae to Mor's car.

Wrae linked arms with Lochlen, and Ferelith did likewise with Mor, and they headed to the car where the men helped them into the back seat.

Lochlen sat in the front passenger seat, and Mor drove them off to the prestigious hotel in Edinburgh where the ball was being held in the large function room.

It was only a short drive to the venue, and soon they were arriving along with numerous other guests. The hotel was aglow with lights, and as Mor and Lochlen escorted Ferelith and Wrae towards the well–lit entrance, the night air was buzzing with excitement.

Everyone was arriving in style, but Ferelith's glittering gold ballgown shone beautifully, as did

Wrae's sparkling lilac ballgown. The fabric of their dresses shimmered under the lights as they walked through the hotel's busy reception and into the function room. Tables were arranged around the edges of the large dance floor.

A member of staff showed the foursome to their table. Although Ferelith had anticipated how spectacular the venue would be, her heart fluttered with excitement, seeing the grandeur and being in the heart of it.

The illusion neckline and sheer sleeves of her ballgown scintillated under the chandeliers, making it look as if she'd been sprinkled with starlight.

Mor leaned close to her. 'You really do look beautiful,' he whispered, causing her to smile and blush slightly.

Wrae and Lochlen were chatting animatedly and looking around at all the guests, having spotted and waved to Huntine who was there with Cambeul. Dair was dancing in his show that evening and wasn't able to join them.

The press were a discreet presence, and photographs were being taken that were due to be highlighted in the news the following day.

The journalist who'd written the magazine feature about Ferelith, Wrae, Lochlen and Mor approached their table with the bright smile.

'Do you mind if I take a picture of you?' the journalist said, setting up his camera to snap a group photo of them.

They were happy to oblige, and he took a picture of them seated at their table, and then requested one where they were standing up.

'Let's show those gorgeous ballgowns to full effect,' the journalist said. 'I'm assuming they are your own designs.'

'They are,' Ferelith confirmed.

'Are any of your dancers here tonight?' the journalist said to Mor.

'No, I was the only one invited,' Mor explained. 'But I'm here with the ladies and Lochlen.'

'I was talking to Huntine Grey when she arrived,' the journalist said to Ferelith and Wrae. 'She told me that you are designing the costumes for her forthcoming stage play.'

'That's correct,' said Wrae. 'We've started work on the costumes.'

The journalist noted their comments, and then left them to enjoy their evening.

It was Mor who noticed two members of the hotel's management having a concerned discussion while gesturing towards their table. 'It looks like there's something going on. The staff keep glancing over at us.'

'They're coming over,' said Lochlen.

Ferelith and Wrae exchanged a concerned glance. Before they had a chance to discuss this, the two managers were standing beside their table. And their focus was on Ferelith.

Mor spoke up. 'Is there something wrong?'

'We have a problem,' one of the managers stated, looking concerned. 'We'd scheduled a concert pianist to play for us this evening as part of the opening announcement of the ball. Unfortunately, the pianist has had to cancel at the last minute due to travel arrangement delays. Guests are expecting a pianist to perform. We've asked around the guests and the only one here this evening capable of playing a classical piece of music is you, Ferelith.'

When he called her by her name, Ferelith jolted.

'We saw in the press that Ferelith played in your eatery, Lochlen, for the first of your ceilidh dancing nights,' the manager added.

'Yes, Ferelith played wonderfully,' said Lochlen.

'My sister plays beautifully,' Wrae added. 'She can play everything from a rhapsody to a concerto.'

Ferelith's heart was thundering, unsure what to do. Playing to such a prestigious and large audience hadn't been part of her plans. Now here she was being encouraged to step up and play the piano. And what a piano it was. A beautiful baby grand piano sat on the stage area. She'd admired it when she arrived, not thinking she'd be asked to play it.

'You play so well,' Mor said to Ferelith.

Five sets of eyes looked hopefully at Ferelith, and taking a deep breath, before she changed her mind, she agreed.

'Thank you so much,' the manager said, sounding relieved. 'We have a selection of sheet music available. Would you care to pick a piece to play before we make the official opening announcement?' He gestured towards the piano.

Ferelith smiled nervously and stood up.

Wrae gave Ferelith's hand a reassuring squeeze. 'You can do this.'

Mor and Lochlen smiled encouragement.

Ferelith walked over to the stage area, aware of all the eyes on her as the managers accompanied her. Guests did expect someone to play the piano as part of the opening, and a few recognised Ferelith, including Huntine and Cambeul, knowing she could play. Seeing her heading to the piano, a lull descended over the guests as they got ready to listen to her play.

Ferelith overhead a few comments about her ballgown as she walked across the dance floor to the stage area.

'*That's the theatre costume designer who was in the paper...*'

'*I love her gold ballgown, probably one of her own designs...*'

'*She's here with Mor the dancer...*'

'*Mor looks besotted with her...*'

'*Are they dating...?*

'*We should hire her to make the costumes for our next play...*'

'*She's a costume designer and a pianist...*'

'*There's a pink piano in their costume shop...*'

'These are the music sheets we have on hand,' one of the managers said to Ferelith.

She glanced at them and couldn't decide. Her mind was in such a whirl. 'I'll play a medley. I won't need sheet music for that. I'll play part of a sonata, followed by pieces from a well–known concerto and finish with a traditional rhapsody.'

'Excellent,' said the manager. 'We'll leave you to it. Play when you're ready, and then we'll announce the start of the ball.'

Smiling at her, grateful for her help, they walked away, leaving Ferelith to sit down at the piano. And begin...

The melodic sounds of the sonata filtered through the function room, drifting gently, and Ferelith felt the resonance of the notes as she played the beautiful piano. The excitement and joy of playing such a wonderful baby grand piano helped override her initial nervousness. Her performance was one of her best. It was one of those nights when she played with such assurance, rising to the occasion when she needed it.

Rather than be overwhelmed by the challenge of performing, she became lost in the music. The classic sonata was one of her favourite pieces that she'd played over the years, and now it would hold a special place in her memories — the night she played at the ball. She could hear herself create her own little piece of happy history.

Whispers swept through the guests seated at their tables, acknowledging that this was the woman from the press coverage playing the piano, the theatre costume designer who had a pink piano in her shop. Seeing her gold ballgown, particularly the illusion neckline and sleeves glittering under the lights, they applauded her ability and that she'd stepped up into an unfamiliar role this evening to help the proceedings.

Mor's admiration for Ferelith shone clearly. His loving expression reflected the warmth he felt in his heart for her.

Ferelith smoothly merged the sonata section into the concerto. The guests nodded to each other, realising she was playing a medley of pieces rather than the complete sonata. They seemed delighted to hear her now play part of a concerto. Even those unfamiliar with the compositions could hear the change in the music for each piece.

Following the concerto, she played a piece of a popular rhapsody.

Ferelith finished by adding a nocturne, a short romantic piece of piano music that expressed the feelings and atmospheric quality of nighttime. A deeply romantic night. A fitting conclusion to her performance that evening.

When she finished playing, she took a deep breath and looked around at the reaction, at the smiles and applause.

The managers hurried over to Ferelith to thank her, accompanied by a couple of journalists eager to get a few photos and quotes. And Mor was quick to stride over to be by her side, and accompany her back to her table after she'd spoken to the press.

Ferelith went to stand up, but one of the journalists requested a picture of her sitting at the piano with Mor standing beside her.

Several photos were taken quickly so as not to hold up the forthcoming announcement.

'Are you wearing one of your own ballgown designs?' one of the journalists said to her.

'Wrae and I are both wearing our own designs,' Ferelith said as she stepped away from the piano.

The journalists took note of this. One of them had spoken to Huntine Grey on her arrival at the ball, and she'd remarked that the sparkling pink illusion dress she was wearing was one of their designs.

Mor put a protective arm around Ferelith's shoulders to sweep her back to their table.

'Mor, could you give us a quote on Ferelith's performance?' another journalist called to him.

Pausing momentarily, Mor's response was succinct. 'A remarkable performance, from a remarkable woman.'

Happy with this comment, the impromptu press interlude dispersed and the compere for the event stood up on stage and made the opening announcement, welcoming everyone to the ball.

Couples then began to fill the dance floor for the first ballroom waltz of the evening.

'Would you like to dance?' Mor said to Ferelith.

She nodded. 'My heart's still racing.'

So was Mor's. Her loveliness stirred feelings deep inside him that he couldn't deny.

Mor took her in hold and they began to waltz. Ferelith felt wonderful, sweeping around the dance floor wearing the gorgeous ballgown, in Mor's capable arms. And she smiled at Wrae and Lochlen as they waltzed by. Wrae's lilac dress sparkled under the lights.

'You played so well,' Wrae said to her as they danced by each other.

Ferelith smiled at Wrae and Lochlen, and then waltzed on.

Mor swept Ferelith elegantly around the room. The rhythm of the waltz felt wonderful, and their dancing was so in tune that she let him lead her in the next two dances as well. She thought he looked particularly handsome in his smart dinner suit.

Giddy with excitement, and enjoying dancing with Mor, Ferelith finally agreed to take a short break for a refreshing drink and something to eat from the lavish buffet.

Sitting down together at their table, they chatted about the dancing, those present, and then as the music changed to suit a foxtrot, Mor invited Ferelith to join him again on the dance floor.

Taking her in hold, Ferelith felt his gentle strength so close, wrapped around her.

'You're dancing well,' said Mor.

Ferelith giggled. 'This ballgown is hiding a multitude of missteps.'

'Nonsense, you don't feel out of step with me.'

She gazed up at him, wondering if there was more to his comment than polite conversation.

Before she could decide, he whispered instructions to her. 'Lean into the sway. That's it. Hold for a second. And then foxtrot across the diagonal.'

The floor had cleared slightly, giving Mor and Ferelith space for a little bit of display room. Bolstered by her recent lesson, Mor's dance ability, and the remarkable atmosphere of the ball, she enjoyed the stylishness of the dance.

For the first time in a long while, Mor felt in step with every aspect of his life, particularly his dancing, but also on a personal and romantic level. His heart ached to take things further with Ferelith, and perhaps this would be the night when he made his feelings known to her. But even the thought of this, of risking their warm friendship, made him reconsider.

During the evening, Ferelith and Wrae made several new acquaintances in the world of theatre and music with whom they planned to do business.

Mor danced with Huntine, Ferelith danced with Lochlen, and Wrae danced with Cambeul during the ball, as well as with one or two others, though they mainly danced with Mor and Lochlen.

Mor's intensity when dancing the tango with Ferelith ignited feelings in her that were difficult to deny, though she hid them well. Or so she thought. The blush on her cheeks, the sense of passion between them, gave him hope that she had feelings for him as strong as his feelings were for her.

Wrae and Lochlen's tango had more laughter than lust in it. But their close connection was evident.

The fun of the ball matched the splendour of it. Ferelith and Wrae danced well into the night, and as the Cinderella hour approached, they danced the last romantic waltz with Mor and Lochlen.

The lights dimmed to create a romantic atmosphere, and under the sparkling chandeliers, Mor held Ferelith close, wrapping his arms around her. Gazing down at her, the temptation to kiss her was so strong that he almost gave in to the feeling, but held back, wanting her to know that she could completely trust him not to overstep. And certainly not to do it so publicly.

Ferelith's heart reacted to feeling him hold her close, and the shared glance of temptation that sparked between them. It was one of those magical evenings when it would've been easy to give in to the romance of the ball, but she held back too, knowing the time wasn't right. The evening had been memorable, from the unexpected piano performance, to the whole occasion. A perfect night to remember.

As the evening came to a close, everyone began to filter out of the function room and into the night. A sea of car headlights, activity and excited chatter filtered through the air. A great night had been had by all.

Mor and Lochlen escorted Ferelith and Wrae outside and along to where their car was parked nearby. A summer breeze blew through the sparkling fabric of their ballgowns as they hurried along, creating a fairytale feeling as if they were trailing starlight behind them.

Lochlen clasped Wrae's hand, ensuring she didn't trip or falter as they hurried towards the car. The brisk night air was in such contrast to the warmth of the ball, and Mor shielded Ferelith, wrapping his arm around her shoulders.

Reaching the car, Ferelith and Wrae were seated comfortably in the back seat, and then Mor drove them off with Lochlen sitting up front.

'What a fantastic night!' Lochlen exclaimed. 'The dancing, the buffet, and the company made for one of the best nights I've had in a long time.' He glanced round and smiled at Wrae and Ferelith.

'I danced more often than I sat down,' Wrae said, sounding surprised. 'And I thought your ceilidh nights were lively,' she added to Lochlen.

He laughed. 'I can see why you love your ballroom dancing,' Lochlen said to Mor.

'It was a fine evening of dancing,' said Mor. 'Made all the more special dancing with you two,' he added, referring to the ladies.

'I loved that you played the piano,' Wrae exclaimed. 'You're sure to be pictured in the papers.'

Ferelith's heart fluttered with excitement. 'It was such a beautiful piano. I enjoy playing the pink piano, but the baby grand was a treat to play.'

Mor drove through the heart of the city and took Ferelith and Wrae home first, dropping them off at their cottage.

When Mor parked the car, he jumped out, as did Lochlen, and walked the ladies to the front door, seeing them safely inside.

There was a moment of hesitation in their goodnights, but no stolen kisses were exchanged, only warm hugs and smiles at the end of a wonderful night out.

Ferelith and Wrae stood lit up in the doorway of the cottage and waved as the men drove off, then they went inside and closed the door, still buzzing with excitement.

They headed through to their bedrooms, filling the cottage with their chatter.

'I'm excited, but I'm tired,' Ferelith said loud enough that Wrae could hear her. 'And I love this ballgown and really don't want to take it off.' She kicked off her shoes and flopped backwards down on to the bed like a beautifully dressed rag doll.

Wrae's laughter rang through to Ferelith's room. Wrae had reluctantly taken a longing look at herself wearing the lilac ballgown, before taking it off and hanging it up on the outside of the wardrobe. Throwing on a silky robe, and replacing her shoes with fluffy slippers, she padded through to the kitchen.

'I'll make us a cup of tea, or would you prefer a mug of warm milk to soothe you to sleep?' Wrae called through to Ferelith.

'Strong, milky tea,' Ferelith called back, taking a bit of both options.

Hearing the tea being made, Ferelith sighed, thinking about Mor and how close he'd come to kissing her. She was sure he was tempted as much as she was.

Ferelith was still sprawled, all a glitter, on the bed as Wrae came in carrying two mugs of tea. She put one down on the bedside table, and sipped the other while sitting on a chair.

'Did Mor kiss you?' Wrae said, eager to hear what had happened between them.

'No.' Ferelith took a sip of her tea.

'Lochlen and I thought he'd kissed you more than once.'

Ferelith shook her head. 'He came close to kissing me, and I'd be lying if I said I would've resisted him.' She sighed heavily. 'But I just don't want to get inveigled in a summer romance.'

'It's almost autumn,' Wrae teased her.

'You know what I mean.'

'I do.'

'What about you and Lochlen? The pair of you were very cosy. Did he kiss you?'

Wrae tried to contain a smile. 'Maybe.'

'Either you did or you didn't.'

'When we finished dancing a waltz, he leaned down to kiss me on the cheek, but I turned my face, not expecting him to do this, and—'

'You were smooching with Lochlen,' Ferelith concluded.

Wrae didn't deny it. 'It was a ball. I was wearing a fairytale ballgown. It was a romantic night.'

'You minx!'

They burst out laughing.

'So are you and Lochlen dating now?'

'I don't know. I'm just taking things lightly, enjoying the moments, as should you.'

'Maybe I will.' Ferelith washed her fib down with a sip of tea.

'Don't tell lies.'

Ferelith shrugged. 'I've probably missed my moment anyway. The ball is over, and I won't be dancing with Mor again. No dance lessons are scheduled. He was only teaching me so I was ready for the ball. It'll be his show's dress rehearsal next. Followed by his opening night. Then he'll be busy performing at the theatre for a full season.'

'I think you should give romance with Mor a chance,' Wrae encouraged her.

Ferelith didn't commit one way or the other and finished drinking her tea.

'We'd better get some sleep,' said Ferelith.

Wrae nodded, finished her tea and stood up. 'A busy day tomorrow.' The costumes had to be organised and delivered to the theatre for Mor's forthcoming dress rehearsal. And they were both scheduled to attend.

As Wrae went through to her room, Ferelith took her ballgown off, hung it up on the outside of the wardrobe, and got ready for bed.

Lying in bed, Ferelith admired the gold dress sparkling in the night glow streaming through the window. A fairytale ballgown. A fairytale night. But not all fairytales had a happy ever after. Wondering what would happen between her and Mor, she fell sound asleep.

The next couple of days were a whirlwind of costume making, dress designing, and having Mor's costumes delivered to the theatre in Edinburgh for his dance show's full dress rehearsal. Final fittings had been made, and now all that remained was for Ferelith and Wrae to close their shop at five, and drive to the rehearsal at the theatre.

Ferelith, Wrae, Mor and Lochlen had been extra busy recently and any hints of romance following on from the ball had been overtaken by their hectic schedules. But Wrae had invited Lochlen to go with them to see Mor's opening night show, and he'd been pleased to accept.

The ball had been featured in the newspapers, and included pictures of Ferelith sitting at the piano with Mor standing beside her. And pictures showing the guests waltzing on the dance floor that included Wrae and Lochlen. A photo was captioned — *playwright Huntine Grey wears a theatre costume design ballgown.*

The recent publicity had again created interest in the theatre costume design shop.

Locking up the shop for the night, Ferelith and Wrae drove to the theatre. Ferelith wore a floral tea dress from her wardrobe stash, while Wrae opted for a classic shift dress.

The mellow glow of the fading sun cast the theatre in a burnished ambiance as Ferelith and Wrae parked nearby and walked into the classic entrance.

They headed through to the auditorium that was bustling with activity from Mor telling the videographer what he wanted filmed, to his show director talking to Torra, Creag and the other dancers. The lighting was being adjusted and last minute changes made to the stage setting. There was a sense of glamour and romance to the setting, created mainly from the lighting effects casting a varying colourful glow to the stage.

A theatre assistant welcomed Ferelith and Wrae and showed them to their seats. Most of the seats were empty, and they sat down and watched the activity. The theatre had a wardrobe department and two of the staff were assisting the dancers with their costumes. Ferelith and Wrae were on hand to make any necessary alterations to the costumes if needed.

A few minutes later, Mor noticed Ferelith and Wrae sitting there and he came bounding down from the stage to welcome them.

'Thank you for coming along to the rehearsal,' Mor said to them. He wore the red shirt they'd designed and black trousers, and stage makeup that emphasised his handsome features.

'We're looking forward to watching the show,' said Ferelith.

'The stage setting is wonderful, so atmospheric,' Wrae added.

Mor nodded. 'I'm pleased with it.'

'Mor!' His show director beckoned him back up on stage to discuss the opening routine with the other dancers.

'I'll see you both later,' Mor assured them. 'And I'm having the performance filmed by the videographer.' He gestured to where the man and his assistant were set up, both armed with video cameras and sound equipment.

'Mor! We're on in five minutes,' his show director called urgently.

Ferelith and Wrae watched him hurry away and got ready to sit back and watch the dance show. They'd designed and fitted all of the costumes for the eight dancers. Now it was time to enjoy the performance, and see how well the costumes worked when worn for an entire show that included fast costume changes. This would highlight any further design alterations needed before the show's opening night.

Turning their phones off as the main lights in the auditorium dimmed, they gazed up at the stage, and felt a sense of excitement charge the air. The stage lighting created a romantic evening atmosphere, timing in with the music, beaming a starry night sky effect as the show began...

Mor danced on to the stage, leaping in strong, balletic movements.

Ferelith felt her heart react seeing his powerful performance.

From the front stalls, the show was being filmed by the videographer, and Ferelith pictured how wonderful it would be to rewatch the show.

Wrae nudged Ferelith, smiling and nodding. They were both astounded at the high level of the dancing and the whole effect Mor and the others had created. Everything from the choreography and stage direction to the lighting and music were incredible.

And the costumes played their part too, enhancing the dancers' performance, and adding glamour and sparkle to the show.

They smiled at each other when Mor made a quick change off stage and emerged wearing his tartan kilt. The blue sequins shimmered as he danced. The effect was what Ferelith had hoped for, and Wrae gave her a nod, agreeing that it looked great.

There were times when Ferelith was so caught up in the excitement of the show, that she realised she'd been holding her breath. The drama matched the dancing, and she sensed that Mor's show was going to be a huge success.

The first half of the show finished with a dramatic dance routine, involving Mor performing a combination of lifts with Torra, lifting her with ease as she gracefully moved from one position to the next. Creag and the other dancers were backing them, and the entire routine was breathtaking. A great note to end on before the twenty minute interval.

The lights in the auditorium rose slightly, while maintaining the atmosphere.

Although there was no audience as such, the plan was to use the dress rehearsal exactly as it would be timed during the live audience performances.

The dancers went backstage to change their costumes, and have refreshments, and generally get ready for the second half. The show director joined them.

Instead of going backstage with them, Mor made a bold decision, one that he'd been thinking about since the night of the ball. His heart thundered as he jumped down from the stage and hurried towards Ferelith and Wrae. His shirt was unbuttoned, exposing his lean abs, and his broad shoulders seemed to be carrying the weight of something troubling him.

The tense expression on his face indicated that something was wrong. They assumed it was with the costumes, but they were mistaken.

His dramatic stage makeup emphasised his fabulous blue eyes and there was stray glitter sparkling in his thick, blond hair.

Mor looked down at them, and clasped Ferelith's hand with an urgency she didn't resist.

'I need to talk to you,' Mor said to Ferelith in a tone that sounded so intense it sent a flurry of butterflies through her.

Nodding politely to Wrae, Mor led Ferelith away and up on to the side of the stage where they stood on their own. He clearly wanted a moment to speak to her in the nearest to private as he was able under the circumstances. The dancers and others were all backstage, and Mor and Ferelith's moment was lit by a glittering night sky effect above them.

'What's wrong, Mor?' she said, keeping her voice down.

His handsome face looked like he belonged to a fantasy world where shimmering sparkle had rained down and sprinkled light on every sculptured contour. And the blue of his eyes was the most intense she'd ever seen.

He kept a hold of her hand, as if he never wanted to let her go, and took a steadying breath, so deep and strong it showed in the breadth of his shoulders.

'I have to tell you something,' he began. 'Since the day I first met you in the costume shop, I've felt a love for you that I can no longer hide.'

Ferelith felt a wave of emotion sweep through her as she continued to listen.

'I know that neither of us was looking for romance, but I've found myself falling in love with you, and I hope that you'll take a chance on me, on us.'

Ferelith's smile warmed his heart, giving him the hope he'd been longing for.

His strong arms pulled her close to him gently, and he leaned down and kissed her.

Mor's kiss ignited the feelings she'd been trying to resist.

'We can make this work, Ferelith. I know we can. I love you so much,' he said, gazing down at her.

'We will,' she said, hearing the emotion in her voice, and the love in her heart for this wonderful man.

Mor kissed her again, and again, until her excited laughter made him pause, and they realised they had an audience of the dancers watching them. The twenty minute interval was almost done, but they'd become so steeped in their romantic moments that they hadn't noticed.

Ferelith blushed as Mor put his arm around her and hurried with her to the steps at the side of the stage. With her thoughts and feelings in a whirl, she hesitated for a moment, and Mor took charge of her, lifting her up and carrying her back to her seat. She put her arm around his shoulders, feeling the strong muscles beneath the sheer fabric of his shirt, and smiled, giddy with excitement.

Wrae had seen a glimpse of what had happened, and smiled with glee, so happy for them.

Mor placed Ferelith down in her seat, and stepped away, then stepped back and kissed her. Then he hurried back up, leaping on to the stage like a man filled with energy and joy.

The lights in the auditorium dimmed again, and the second half of the show began...

Wrae squeezed Ferelith's hand. 'I'm so happy for you.' She gave her sister a hug, and then they settled down to watch the show.

Mor had given an energetic performance for the first half. But he now had extra vigour, spinning, leaping across the stage, performing the lifts with stylish ease, and shining with such star quality that the energy would surely transfer to the video.

Ferelith watched in awe, and now with a different future to look forward to. One with this incredible man.

The show concluded on a spectacular note, and the dancers took their bow and smiled out into the auditorium, anticipating audiences reaction when the live show started soon.

With her heart filled with love and joy, Ferelith waved to Mor, leaving him to discuss the performance with the dancers and his show director.

As she walked away with Wrae, she glanced back towards the stage, and there was Mor watching her, smiling and waving to her.

Ferelith waved back at him, sensing that her world was about to change, a change for the better she was sure.

The opening night of Mor's dance show was a grand affair.

The classic theatre was lit up in the night. Hundreds of people poured in, chatting excitedly, and seated themselves in the auditorium that had various seating levels, including a balcony and box seats high up on either side of the stage. The tickets for the show were sold out.

Ferelith and Wrae were seated in the front stalls with a great view of the stage. Lochlen sat beside Wrae, and beside them were their grandparents and parents, along with Efie and her husband. Huntine Grey was there too with Dair the dancer, who'd managed to get a night off from his dance tour, and Cambeul. Everyone was well–dressed.

'I'm so excited,' Ferelith confided to Wrae. 'I can't imagine how keyed–up Mor and the dancers must be.'

Wrae smiled at her and whispered. 'I'm glad our parents and grandparents are here. I think they're in for a treat when they see this show.'

Ferelith nodded, and then they settled down as the lights dimmed, the curtain rose, the music played, and Mor and the dancers began to perform...

'What a show!' Ferelith and Wrae's grandmother exclaimed as the curtain came down at the end of the night. Their grandfather agreed.

'Your costume designs were wonderful,' their father acknowledged.

Their mother wholeheartedly agreed. 'An excellent use of the fabric, particularly for the dresses and ballgowns.'

'And that red shirt Mor was wearing was flashy but fashionable,' their father remarked. 'I liked it.'

'We'll make one for you,' Ferelith joked with her father.

He tilted his head and grinned. 'I might take you up on that offer.' He turned to his wife. 'What do you think?'

'Only if Wrae and Ferelith make me an evening dress to match from that gorgeous chiffon,' their mother said, half joking, half wanting one.

Ferelith nodded firmly. 'Consider it done.'

Their laughter and chatter continued as they all made their way backstage, showing their meet and greet tickets to the theatre staff.

Efie squeezed her husband's arm in anticipation of meeting all the dancers and having photos taken with them.

The meet and greet was well underway with other members of the audience delighted to have a picture taken with Mor, Torra, Creag and the others.

Mor kept smiling at Ferelith, assuring her that he'd be able to give her his full attention once the meet and greet was finished. He loved meeting members of the audience, as did the other dancers, and this created a happy atmosphere to round off the show night.

But the night was far from over. It was about to begin, backstage, with the entire show crew and invited friends.

Mor made a beeline for Ferelith, and kissed her. Loving and passionate.

'The show was wonderful,' she told him.

He smiled at her and kissed her again.

After she introduced her grandparents and parents to Mor and the others, champagne was popped and everyone drank a toast to the successful opening night.

And then the music started, a lively mix of songs to get everyone in the party mood and up and dancing.

Lochlen attempted a bit of ceilidh dancing, and was surprised when everyone joined in, laughing, all having fun together.

'I didn't know Dad could dance like that,' Wrae whispered to Ferelith.

'Or Mum,' Ferelith added.

Then they smiled watching their grandparents giving it large.

Wrae was then swept into the reel by Lochlen.

Somewhere in the energetic dancing, Mor wrapped Ferelith in his arms, and kissed her, assuring her that they had a happy and exciting future to look forward to.

In that romantic moment with Mor, Ferelith sensed she'd found her happy ever after with all the people she loved, and that she was now part of Mor's world, of dancing, music and romance.

End

About the Author:

De-ann Black is a bestselling author, scriptwriter and former newspaper journalist. She has over 100 books published. Romance, thrillers, espionage novels, action adventure. And children's books (non-fiction rocket science books and children's fiction). She became an Amazon All-Star author in 2014 and 2015.

She previously worked as a full-time newspaper journalist for several years. She had her own weekly columns in the press. This included being a motoring correspondent where she got to test drive cars every week for the press for three years.

Before being asked to work for the press, De-ann worked in magazine editorial writing everything from fashion features to social news. She was the marketing editor of a glossy magazine.

She is also a professional artist and illustrator. Embroidery design, fabric design, dressmaking, sewing, knitting and fashion are part of her work.

Additionally, De-ann has always been interested in fitness, and was a fitness and bodybuilding champion, 100 metre runner and mountaineer. As a former N.A.B.B.A. Miss Scotland, she had a weekly fitness show on the radio that ran for over three years.

De-ann trained in Shukokai karate, boxing, kickboxing, Dayan Qigong and Jiu Jitsu. She is currently based in Scotland.

Her 16 colouring books are available in paperback, including her latest Summer Nature Colouring Book and Flower Nature Colouring Book.

Her latest embroidery pattern books include: Floral Garden Embroidery Patterns, Christmas & Winter Embroidery Patterns, Floral Spring Embroidery Patterns and Sea Theme Embroidery Patterns.

Website: Find out more at: www.de-annblack.com

Fabric, Wallpaper & Home Decor Collections:
De-ann's fabric designs and wallpaper collections, and home decor items, including her popular Scottish Garden Thistles patterns, are available from Spoonflower.
www.de-annblack.com/spoonflower

Also by De-ann Black (Romance, Action/Thrillers & Children's books). See her Amazon Author page or website for further details about her books, screenplays, illustrations, art, fabric designs and embroidery patterns.

Amazon Author page:
www.De-annBlack.com/Amazon

Romance books:

Dance, Music & Scottish Romance series:
1. Romance Dancer

Quilt Shop by the Seaside
Embroidery Bee

Scottish Loch Romance series:
1. Sewing & Mending Cottage
2. Scottish Loch Summer Romance
3. Sweet Music
4. Knitting Bee
5. Autumn Romance
6. Christmas Ballroom Dancing
7. Scottish Highlands New Year Ball
8. Crafting Bee: Crafts & Romance in Scotland

Music, Dance & Romance series:
1. The Sweetest Waltz
2. Knitting & Starlight
3. Ballroom Dancing Christmas Romance

Snow Bells Haven series:
1. Snow Bells Christmas
2. Snow Bells Wedding
3. Love & Lyrics

The Cure for Love Romance series:
1. The Cure for Love
2. The Cure for Love at Christmas

Scottish Highlands & Island Romance series:
1. Scottish Island Knitting Bee
2. Scottish Island Fairytale Castle
3. Vintage Dress Shop on the Island
4. Fairytale Christmas on the Island
5. Summer Ball Weddings & Waltzing

Quilting Bee & Tea Shop series:
1. The Quilting Bee
2. The Tea Shop by the Sea
3. Embroidery Cottage
4. Knitting Shop by the Sea
5. Christmas Weddings

Sewing, Crafts & Quilting series:
1. The Sewing Bee
2. The Sewing Shop
3. Knitting Cottage (Scottish Highland romance)
4. Scottish Highlands Christmas Wedding

Cottages, Cakes & Crafts series:
1. The Flower Hunter's Cottage
2. The Sewing Bee by the Sea
3. The Beemaster's Cottage
4. The Chocolatier's Cottage
5. The Bookshop by the Seaside
6. The Dressmaker's Cottage

Scottish Chateau, Colouring & Crafts series:
1. Christmas Cake Chateau
2. Colouring Book Cottage

Summer Sewing Bee

Sewing, Knitting & Baking series:
1. The Tea Shop
2. The Sewing Bee & Afternoon Tea
3. The Christmas Knitting Bee
4. Champagne Chic Lemonade Money
5. The Vintage Sewing & Knitting Bee

Tea Dress Shop series:
1. The Tea Dress Shop At Christmas
2. The Fairytale Tea Dress Shop In Edinburgh
3. The Vintage Tea Dress Shop In Summer

The Tea Shop & Tearoom series:
1. The Christmas Tea Shop & Bakery
2. The Christmas Chocolatier
3. The Chocolate Cake Shop in New York at Christmas
4. The Bakery by the Seaside
5. Shed in the City

Christmas Romance series:
1. Christmas Romance in Paris
2. Christmas Romance in Scotland

Oops! I'm the Paparazzi series:
1. Oops! I'm the Paparazzi
2. Oops! I'm Up To Mischief
3. Oops! I'm the Paparazzi, Again

The Bitch-Proof Suit series:
1. The Bitch-Proof Suit
2. The Bitch-Proof Romance
3. The Bitch-Proof Bride
4. The Bitch-Proof Wedding

Heather Park: Regency Romance
Dublin Girl
Why Are All The Good Guys Total Monsters?
I'm Holding Out For A Vampire Boyfriend

Action/Thriller books:

Knight in Miami
Agency Agenda
Love Him Forever
Someone Worse
Electric Shadows
The Strife Of Riley
Shadows Of Murder
Cast a Dark Shadow

Children's books:

Faeriefied
Secondhand Spooks
Poison-Wynd
Wormhole Wynd
Science Fashion
School For Aliens

Colouring books:

Summer Nature
Flower Nature
Summer Garden
Spring Garden
Autumn Garden
Sea Dream
Festive Christmas
Christmas Garden
Christmas Theme
Flower Bee
Wild Garden
Faerie Garden Spring
Flower Hunter
Stargazer Space
Bee Garden
Scottish Garden Seasons

Embroidery Design books:

Floral Garden Embroidery Patterns
Floral Spring Embroidery Patterns
Christmas & Winter Embroidery Patterns
Sea Theme Embroidery Patterns
Floral Nature Embroidery Designs
Scottish Garden Embroidery Designs

Printed in Dunstable, United Kingdom